I0721991

SINISTER LANG SYNE

A SHORT WICKS HOLLOW NOVEL

COLLEEN GLEASON

PROLOGUE

New Year's Eve 1929

IT WAS A BRISK, snapping cold night to celebrate the ring-ing-in of the new year—a new decade that many hoped would eventually see the end of the Eighteenth Amendment.

Despite Prohibition, however, the people of tiny Wicks Hollow village held glasses of champagne, mugs of beer, and bottles of whisky as they thronged in front of the Tremaine Clock Tower. Being situated near Lake Michigan on the shipping route from Canada to Chicago meant that residents of the small town had easy access to shipments of the illegal beverages.

Women wearing the flimsy, loose flapper-style dresses currently in fashion covered themselves with heavy wool coats and jaunty cloches over cropped-short hair, with gloved hands gripping their drinks as they jostled in the crowd. Their companions, men in heavy coats and trilbies, fedoras, or Homburgs, bundled the women closer against the crisp bitter cold and helped to keep them warm.

White clouds of breath mingled and meshed as a hundred people talked, sang, and laughed in the midst of their small, close-knit town. It was a night of celebration for many reasons.

They gathered below the wrought iron balcony of the brand new Tremaine Clock Tower, where Miss Brenda Tremaine, the town's most famous socialite, was about to marry the handsome and debonair State Senator Barclay Langford beneath a starry winter sky. Their vows would be made as soon as the clock struck midnight.

Despite an ugly scene between Senator Langford and his former love, Lonna Dunne, last week, the bride and groom were happy and excited with eyes glowing and cheeks pink from the chill. Nothing would stop them from sealing their wedding vows—not even a crazed, wild-eyed woman and her threats of curses.

The construction of the Tremaine Tower—overseen by Tremaine Construction with the help of Wicks Development —had been completed only two weeks earlier, and tonight was its inaugural event. Imposing and elegant, the dark brick building boasted a large, three-sided clock face, which could be seen from over a mile away. Above the clock was the bell tower, with seven bells prepared to ring in the New Year and the marital junction of the powerful Langford and Tremaine families. Extending from the top of the bell tower was a short spire where a glittering ball perched. The ball would burst into sparkling light on the twelfth stroke of midnight as the crowd watched and celebrated the entry into a new decade.

Brenda and Barclay stood on the balcony below the clock,

waving to their friends and family. A large banner with their logo for the celebration—two ornate, intertwined Bs above a framed *January 1, 1930*—fluttered from the iron railing in front of them.

Despite the chill, Brenda had donned neither coat nor hat nor gloves to spoil her appearance. Slender and boyish in figure—as most of the women of the time aspired to be—she wore a stunning champagne colored dress that glittered with beads of silver, white, pale gold, and ice pink. Frothy, delicate feathers shivered from her shoulders with every movement, and the gown fell in a straight, unbroken line to just the tops of her knees. A large brooch sporting a half-dollar-sized crystal of pale rose surrounded by more feathers glinted from the center of her gown. Her short blond hair, crimped into finger waves, was held in place by glittering pins, and a headband with more gems and feathers cut across her creamy white forehead.

She held the stem of a broad, shallow glass filled with the dark red cranberry champagne cocktail she'd asked to be created specially for her wedding. In the room behind the balcony waited a small and elegant reception with a champagne fountain spilling with the same cranberry bubbles, and trays of tiny shrimp sandwiches, fruit kebabs, and minuscule pastries.

"Brenda! You're going to catch your death!" cried one of her friends from the ground below. "Put on a coat!"

"I'm not the least bit chilled," the bride called back, leaning over the railing with a smile. "I'm ablaze with the warmth of love!"

Her groom was just as handsomely attired in a creamy-white jacket with tails. His tie was also festooned with sparkling gems and sequins, and his dark blond hair was slicked back from a

clean-shaven face. He crowded behind her at the railing, wrapping both arms around the bride and offering her his warmth.

"It's nearly midnight!" someone cried, and everyone's attention turned from the gorgeous bride and groom to the massive clock face above them. "Three minutes!"

"Are you ready, my love?" said Barclay, turning his bride to face him.

"So very ready," she replied, looking up with a smile.

She had no worries about Lonna Dunne and her mad threats. Despite the madwoman's ugly words, there was no such thing as a curse!

Barclay bent to kiss her, then they turned together to watch the last two minutes tick on the clock above them.

They made a pretty picture: the pair of gleaming blond heads, their willowy champagne-colored figures as they stood with their backs to the audience, looking up at the clock, drinks in hands ready to toast the new year.

"Ten...*nine!...eight!*" chanted the onlookers. "Seven! Six!"

Brenda looked at Barclay and said something no one on the ground could hear. He smiled lovingly at her, and they both turned to face each other beneath the clock as the count-down continued. It made a stunning picture, and many flash-bulbs went off as they captured the iconic moment.

"Five...four...*three!...two!...ONE!*"

Above, a single bell in the steeple began to bong the twelve tolls for the hour just as the silvery ball atop it exploded into life. Lit, glittering, glowing, the ball dropped.

And then someone screamed.

"Brenda!"

"Oh my God!"

"What's happened?"

"Brenda!"

Barclay Langford, the stunned bridegroom, stared down at the crumpled form of his bride...an unmoving pile of sparkling fabric and awkward limbs on the balcony next to him.

The broken champagne glass glittered on the balcony next to her, and the dark red cocktail had splattered all over her face and the front of her frock.

She was dead.

CHAPTER 1

Present Day

THE LAST TIME Callie Quigley had been inside the Tremaine Tower was when she was sixteen.

On New Year's Eve.

Just before midnight.

That was sixteen years ago, and it had been a *memorable* night...in more ways than one.

And there were parts she definitely didn't want to repeat.

And yet, here I am.

She chuckled nervously and pushed against the heavy door. *Too late to back out now.*

The door creaked and protested, swinging open with great reluctance to reveal the stairs that wound up to the clock tower's only chamber.

The metal steps rang dully as she climbed, her boots making solid sounds with each step. She hoped the noise would scare away anything that might lurk inside the tower... whether it be of the furry, scuttling sort or the darting, wing-thwacking kind.

She was *not* going to think about the wispy, ghostly type.

The Curse of the Tremaine Clock Tower was well-known among the residents of Wicks Hollow—about how Brenda Tremaine had been cursed by her fiancé's former lover, and how she'd dropped dead on the twelfth stroke of midnight—just before making her wedding vows.

But that event alone hadn't been enough to cement the story of the curse. There'd been several other strange and sudden deaths over the years since December 31, 1929.

All on New Year's Eve.

All during weddings.

All unexplained.

All cursed.

Callie shivered a little, and not just because it was mid-December in Michigan near one of the Great Lakes.

Why did I decide to do this again...?

Because CQEvents is going to be one of the premier wedding planners in West Michigan and this is a great marketing move.

At the top of the stairs, she found herself on a spare landing with a door that she knew opened into a small room, along with dust motes, cobwebs, and piles of other stuff she didn't care to examine too closely.

The lock to the room was a little cranky, but the key she'd been given eventually turned, and she pushed open the door.

Sixteen years hadn't changed much about the place—including the fact that it was still as shadowy, dank, and eerie as she remembered from that fateful night.

Callie walked over the threshold, her breath making short, compact white puffs in the chill air. The small room—which was hardly more than a waiting area for the Clock Tower's extravagant balcony—had two large windows on either side and was cast in the long shadows of a late afternoon in December.

A few straight-backed chairs were angled around a low table, and Callie wondered if they'd even been moved since she and Ben and the others had high-tailed it out of there that night. Some dusty bottles—including one still lying in the center of the table from their Spin the Bottle Truth or Dare game—littered the floor.

They'd been there to celebrate the New Year while "braving" the Curse of Tremaine Tower...and to have a few bottles of champagne and a little bit of weed, unseen by their parents. Ben brought his iPod and portable speaker, but they dared not play the music too loudly for fear they'd be discovered inside what was supposed to be a dark and empty building beneath the illuminated clock face.

They'd reveled in the idea of being in the tower when the clock struck midnight and the ball lit up above it, unseen by the crowds of people that would gather in the square below.

So, in anticipation of the big moment, the seven of them had gathered around the low table, listened to music, spun the bottle...and waited to see what would happen with the curse.

"What a stupid thing to do," she said aloud now, needing to hear something other than the rustling of vermin—mice, she hoped, and not rats—and the creepy clattering of a tree branch against one of the windows.

Thud.

Callie stifled a gasp as she spun around. No one was there, nothing had moved...

"Stop it," she told herself sharply. Aloud again. "You're being—"

Thud, thud, thud...

Now she recognized the dull, ringing sound of boots or shoes as they ascended the metal stairway.

Okay, okay, it's just the caretaker, she told herself. They said he'd stop by to make sure everything was all right.

"Hello?" she called in a jaunty voice, but she curled her fingers around the can of pepper spray on her keyring. It didn't hurt to be too careful nowadays.

Especially in an abandoned building.

"Yo," returned a deep voice as the clanging sound drew nearer. "Everything all right up there?"

"Yes, I—Ben?" She goggled when her old friend came into view at the doorway. It actually took her a second to recognize him, because he'd grown a beard and mustache since she'd last seen him a couple years ago.

"Callie? Is that you?" He stepped onto the landing as she backed up into the ante room once more. "Hi."

She was suddenly, wildly relieved she hadn't taken off her hat, and that the deep blue slouch—which she was fully aware made her eyes look bluer than blue—was keeping her wild, bright-penny-colored hair under control. With static electricity and the dry winter air, an unhatted head would make her look like she'd stuck her finger in a socket—or like a too-curvy candle with a flame on top. "Wow, Ben...it's been a long time. Are you the caretaker here?"

He was wearing a hat against the winter cold as well—a stone gray beanie that sat just above his dark blond brows—

but unlike Callie, no gloves or boots and only what looked to her like an impractically light athletic jacket. And the short beard, which...wow. It looked *really* good on him. "No—the caretaker's off for the weekend. So when I heard someone was coming in to check out the tower, I volunteered to be the one to check on things."

He stood there, ungloved hands on his hips, and looked at her as if he wasn't sure what to make of the situation.

"Right. That makes sense. After all, your family still partly owns the place, I guess." She felt like she was babbling even though she'd only said a few phrases, and so she clamped her mouth closed and reminded herself that *silence is power*.

That was one of the first things she'd learned in the business world: be quiet and let the other person speak.

Ben Tremaine looked around the room, then walked casually to the door that opened onto the infamous balcony. But he didn't open it. Instead, he circled around and brushed a hand lightly over the back of one of the chairs. He seemed just as uncomfortable as Callie felt...which wasn't all that surprising, considering what happened the last time they were in this room.

She swallowed hard and glanced over to where Frida had laughingly hung up the mistletoe all those years ago. Her eyes widened.

It was still there.

Tattered, dusty, chewed on...but still hanging there.

Callie yanked her eyes away and her attention bounced around the room, touching on the two paintings that hung on the walls and finally the tattered curtains that swagged the pair of windows.

"Uh...so what exactly are you planning to do...here?" Ben asked after the silence stretched.

"I'm having a wedding."

His attention snapped to her. "You're having a wedding? Here?"

"On New Year's Eve." Even as she said those words—strongly, boldly; as if she were tossing down a gauntlet—Callie felt something move in the air. A wisp of hair that had escaped from its fuzzy blue covering buffeted her cheek, giving proof that the sudden waft wasn't her imagination.

Her breath puffed out in a white cloud, much more solid and dark than it had been a moment ago.

Ben's breath was doing the same.

And it felt a lot colder all of a sudden.

Their eyes met across the shadowy space as the air eddied around them. A few crisp leaves—how they'd come to be in here, Callie didn't know—tumbled and swirled on the floor.

"At midnight," she said, figuring she might as well go all the way. "The wedding will be at midnight on New Year's E—"

Something crashed behind her, and she spun around as Ben bolted toward her, nearly flying across the room to get to her side.

The large picture that had been hanging on the wall had fallen.

Even though the painting had landed facedown, Callie already knew whose portrait it was.

Brenda Tremaine.

She and Ben stood next to each other without touching—but close enough that she could feel his warmth—breaths heavy and white as they looked at the painting. She refused, absolutely *refused*, to look at the aged plastic mistletoe that hung just a few feet away.

"It was old," Ben said after a minute. "The wood, the hanger, the string. Something must have just, you know, collapsed after all these years."

Callie, who'd grown up reading her mother's Nancy Drew and Trixie Belden mysteries, was skeptical. She'd long released the pepper spray from her fist, but now she dug in the deep pocket of her long down coat to pull out her phone.

Swiping on the phone's flashlight, she went over to the painting to examine it. Her breath no longer clouded up quite as white, and whatever she had felt in the air seemed to have gone. It was just her and Ben Tremaine, a bunch of vermin (please don't let it be rats) (or bats), and a painting that had just fallen off the wall at an eerily opportune moment.

"The hanger looks completely intact," she said in a neutral voice as she skimmed the light over the back of the painting and pulled on the wire with a gloved finger. "It's made from wire and though it's a little rusty, it's not broken or even bent." She looked up at Ben, who hovered over her.

"I'll check the wall," he said, pulling out his own phone for the light.

Callie didn't stand back while he did the examination. She wanted to make sure it was done to Trixie's standards, so she joined him at the wall where the painting had hung. She shined her own light over the mildewed and stained wallpaper as they edged right up to the wall, their two beams mingling like the clouds of their breath. She could smell faint mint coming from Ben, they were that close, and Callie was *very* glad she'd eschewed the cup of coffee she'd considered earlier and had had lemon-flavored sparkling water instead.

"Looks intact to me," she said needlessly as they both stared at the two nails that had held up the heavy painting. Both protruded from the wall and were angled slightly upright. When Ben tried to jiggle each of them, neither were loose.

"All right, then," he said in a quiet voice.

Callie didn't have anything else to add. There was no way the painting had just *fallen* from the wall.

Her heart was thudding hard and she wasn't certain whether it was because she'd been standing so close to Ben, or because of the creepy things happening.

She stepped back and tucked her phone away. And, just in time, she stopped herself from running a hand through her hair, remembering how wild it would look if she pushed off her hat.

Not that it mattered.

Other than that one time she and Ben had kissed—thanks to the mistletoe she was still absolutely not looking at— nothing else had ever happened between them...at least in that way.

They'd been friends, sure, and they'd spent a lot of time together with their group of nerdy compatriots, but that was it. Other than a few spicy conversations about whether Legolas and Eowyn would have made a good couple, and why on earth *Firefly* had been cancelled—complete with whether Mal and Inara ever got together—everything had been definite "friend zone."

"Well," Ben said after a minute. "Are you done here?"

"I should check out the balcony," she said, suddenly

feeling the chill despite her heavy coat. "After all, that's where the magic" —she gave an awkward chuckle— "is going to happen. But you don't have to stay. I promise to lock up when I'm done."

"It's getting dark pretty quick," he replied. "Probably best if I stick around, just in case."

She gave him a little frowny sort of look. "I'm not afraid of the dark."

"It's dangerous to be poking around in the dark in an unfamiliar place. Especially one that hasn't been used for decades," he said mildly.

"I thought you had a caretaker," she said, walking with firm, confident steps to the balcony's door. "Though it really doesn't look like he does much caretaking."

"*She* does just fine," Ben replied again in that same easy voice. "But her responsibility is really only to make sure the clock and bells—and the New Year's Eve light-up ball, too—work. Since the rest of the building is unusable."

"Which is something I plan to change," Callie said breezily and she turned the knob.

To her surprise and pleasure, the door opened easily and she pushed it wide. The generous expanse of the balcony lay before her, and she stepped out into the wintry air.

A few inches of snow covered the wooden-slatted floor and ornate wrought iron railing. The roofless balcony jutted out in a half-moon shape from one side of the triangular Tremaine Tower building, with the twelve-foot wide clock face only a few feet above. The clock had three sides, and the bell's cupola was in a peaked-roofed top just above it. The silvery glittering ball that exploded with light every New Year's Eve sat on the very pointed tip of the cupola.

Callie walked to the railing and stood there, looking out over the quaint village of Wicks Hollow. She was only twenty feet above the ground, which was why this was a usable location for a wedding—the guests would be below, and a small reception would take place inside the building afterward.

The small town of Wicks Hollow was relatively quiet in December, although tourists did come in from Chicago, Detroit, or Grand Rapids for "holiday shopping" weekends. Many of the local shops offered unique and artisan items, and the town was always dressed to the nines, so to speak, in holiday decor starting the week before Thanksgiving. The tourists stayed in Victorian homes turned into bed-and-breakfasts decorated with fresh greenery, candles, and acres of ribbons and garlands.

Orbra's Tea House also did a healthy business during December for (mostly) ladies who wanted "Holiday Tea" with their friends, sisters, daughters, mothers and so on.

But it was late in the afternoon—just after five—and already the sun had mostly disappeared behind the Lake Michigan horizon. Callie could make out the lake's black water rippling just beyond the westernmost row of houses, shops, and trees. The small marina was closed for the season, but since the trees had dropped their leaves, she could see the broad and deep expanse of the lake, and the Stony Cape Lighthouse just to the north. The sky was dark blue and the lake was inky, with the horizon being only a blush of pale blue in the wake of the setting sun.

Holiday lights in combinations of green and red and blue and white decorated the lampposts throughout the town— green and red on Pamela Boulevard, and blue and white on Faith Avenue. Massive urns spilling with holly, spruce, and fake poinsettias dotted each corner, and wreaths adorned every streetlamp.

In the center of town, just beyond a small park from Tremaine Tower, grew a thirty-foot pine tree that was kept trimmed into a perfect elongated triangle shape. It had been decorated with white and green glittering lights, stars, and reams upon reams of silver and gold garlands. A sparkling three-dimensional star sat on the top branch. Streaks of tinsel and glitter lights arched from each tip of the star, bouncing and dancing in the breeze.

Below, tourists and villagers walked along the streets carrying shopping bags, pushing strollers, managing leashed dogs, and holding hands with loved ones. The little flurry of snowflakes made it look like the consummate festive winter scene.

Callie sighed. This was going to be the perfect place for a wintry, outdoor wedding. She understood why Brenda and Barclay—and the others who'd tragically followed—had chosen the venue originally.

Cursed. They were all cursed. What makes you think anything will be different now?

Her breath came out in quick, foggy little puffs—less substantial than those inside the building—and she knew the tip of her nose had turned bright red from the nip in the air.

What if she was wrong? What if her idea backfired and ended up being a public relations nightmare instead of a brilliant marketing move?

She started a little when Ben came up from behind and moved to stand next to her at the railing, resting his elbows on top as he leaned forward. "Nice view," he said.

"It's like a miniature of the balcony at Buckingham

Palace—you know, where all the royal couples stand after their weddings and kiss for the throngs of people below." There she was, babbling again.

"And like the pope's balcony at St. Peter's Square. But, as you say, smaller."

She smiled, and the shape of her breath-puff changed. "That's right. You get it. It's just a shame so many unfortunate things happened here."

Ben made a noise like he was about to say something then changed his mind. "Well, have you seen enough?"

"I guess so," she replied, wondering why he insisted on staying here with her. She was perfectly capable of checking out a wedding venue all by herself. After all, that was her job.

He stepped back from the rail but seemed to be waiting for her to precede him off the balcony and into the room. Callie decided to acquiesce. He was right—it was getting too dark for her to be bumbling around in an unfamiliar building. And she'd missed lunch because an appointment with a potential new client back in Grand Rapids had gone long, and then she drove down here to pick up the key for the building.

"I'm heading to Uncle Trib's restaurant," she heard herself say as Ben opened the door to the landing and gestured her through. "I'd love to buy you a drink and, you know, maybe catch up on things? I'd love to hear your thoughts on Tom Holland's Spiderman."

"Oh, thanks a lot, but I'd better not. Not tonight. I've got some stuff to do," he said hurriedly. "End of year is coming sooner than you think. Thanks anyway, Callie."

It was a good thing it was dark in the stairwell so Ben couldn't see the high, hot flags of color she knew burned on her cheeks. Well, that was pretty blunt and final and she should have just kept her mouth shut.

At the bottom of the steps she sailed out of the building, then turned and waited for Ben to exit so she could lock up. She was glad to have something to focus on instead of having to look at him. "All right, thanks a lot for stopping by," she said, taking her time with the lock.

"It was really nice to see you again, Callie," he said as she finished turning the key. "I—uh—hope your wedding goes well. Merry Christmas."

And then he walked off across the square, shoulders hunched against the sudden, stiff breeze.

CHAPTER 2

STUPID. Stupid. Stupid.

Ben called himself that and worse as he stalked away from Callie, striding across the snow-covered green toward the downtown area.

He should have *known* she was taken, that some guy had snatched her up and was going to—as they say—put a ring on it.

But when he'd heard Callie Quigley wanted to look at the old Tremaine Tower building, that she was going to be back in town for a project there, he carefully manipulated things so he could be the one to be there when she did.

He hoped like hell that the fact he'd carried a torch for her for eighteen years—hell, more than eighteen years, because it had started when they were *six* when he first caught sight of her bright copper pigtails—hadn't shone like a beacon from his face. Especially once he realized she was back in town not just to visit, but *to get married.*

On New Year's Eve.

In the very same place they'd done what he'd wanted to

do since he was old enough to realize girls weren't gross. Especially Callie Quigley.

Ugh.

Ben scrubbed his face with a hand, feeling the rough bristles of the beard he'd recently decided to grow, even though CPAs didn't wear beards. Probably made him look like a creeper.

Stupid. Stupid. Stupid.

And then she'd invited him for a drink, for Pete's sake.

That would have just been torture, sitting across from her soon-to-be-married self—or, worse, *next* to her if they sat at the bar—and trying to keep from looking at her. To keep from *looking* at her or brushing against her, to keep his gaze from getting caught by those bright, enthusiastic eyes, or getting trapped in one of their friendly debates about superhero movies and watching her get all passionate and worked up.

At least she'd been wearing a big bulky coat that hid all those bodacious curves he assumed—hoped—she still had.

Not that it mattered if she still was as round and soft and luscious as he remembered.

Her eyes had been really blue tonight. Had they always been that blue? Had her mouth always looked so full and pink and luscious?

Yes. Oh, yes, it had, and he had the memory—the experience—to prove it, as the damned mistletoe that *still* hung there in the clock tower room had reminded him.

He'd seen the stupid plastic sphere of greenery with its formerly pearl-colored balls almost the moment he stepped into the room. He couldn't believe it was still hanging there from sixteen years ago. Horrified, he'd yanked his attention away immediately and hoped Callie wouldn't, one, notice it herself, and, two, notice *him* looking at it.

And then that weird thing happened with the painting falling down, and he'd practically thrown himself at her...for what reason? To protect her? From what?

Argh. *Doofus.*

And when they were crowding up next to each other to examine the wall, he'd been close enough to smell her hair or whatever perfume she'd been wearing. The deliciousness of the scent went straight to his hormones. And elsewhere.

Thank God he'd popped a couple mints before he walked over from the office.

He stomped along until he found himself back on Pamela Ave...and he walked right by Trib's, which was already crowded even though it was just after five. He didn't even glance inside to see whether he spotted Callie and her bright hair.

And there was no way he was going to go in there any time in the near future, even though he was Trib's accountant and the guy always comped him a beer or two—and last April, a whole five-course meal with the best steak he'd ever had after Ben had finished the restaurant's taxes and they weren't nearly as painful as Trib had feared.

No, this was a night for The Roost, Ben decided on the spot —instead of going back to the office like he probably should. And it was Tuesday, so that meant Dec and Baxter—and maybe even Jake, if he wasn't on call—would be there for Trivia Night.

The scrawny, dingy bar was the diviest dive in the county with the longest beer list (draft and bottle) and the best burgers and other bar food. They even made great omelettes.

And because it was Trivia Night, Ben—the self-proclaimed Trivia King—would be distracted from thinking about Callie Quigley sitting her delicious self at Trib's only a half a block away and around the corner.

It was early yet, though, so when he pushed open the door of The Roost and saw Baxter was already sitting at the bar, Ben smiled with relief. And the smile widened when he saw that his friend had a cardboard box filled with brown bottles on the counter in front of him.

Yes. That meant Baxter had brought in some samples of his latest brews.

Excellent consolation prize, my man, Ben told himself. Far better than going back to the office and crunching more numbers—though that was what he loved to do. It was a lot easier than talking to people. Especially bright, sunny, interesting people like Callie.

Though the two of them never had a problem finding something to talk about. He particularly liked it when they got into debates about which was better, *Star Wars* or *Star Trek* (*Star Wars*, obviously—which they both agreed on but he liked to play devil's advocate just to wind her up), or whether the seventh season of Buffy actually sucked as much as everyone said it did—except for the last episode.

He particularly liked to rile Callie up about why she was on Team Edward instead of Team Jacob when it was completely obvious to him—even though he'd never read *Twilight*—that Edward was a creepy stalker who would turn off any normal woman. And the guy *glittered*? Really?

Callie's cheeks would get all flushed and her eyes would spark and the words would tumble from her soft pink mouth at the speed of light as she explained why her point of view was the right one.

He *loved* it when she did that.

No, they never had a lack of things to discuss or talk about. It was the getting *beyond* the talking that had been his problem. *Ugh.*

"You're knocking off pretty early on a Tuesday for a man who owns his own business," said Baxter when he saw Ben.

"I caught a whiff of fresh brews in the air, and it lured me in," Ben replied with a pointed look at the unlabeled brown bottles on the bar.

"Well, since your office is across the street, I guess I'll buy that," Baxter said. "I was going to text you anyway because I've got something I want you to try."

"Lay it on me," Ben said, sliding onto a stool next to him. "Hi Kendy," he said to the bartender and manager. She had been his baby-sitter when he was ten.

"Hey, Ben. I promise I'll get you those end of year projections tomorrow," she said with a grimace. "You know how much I *love* doing that kind of stuff. *Not.*" She placed an empty pilsner glass on the counter in front of him. "You're going to like Bax's latest."

"It's a maple sugar stout with coffee overtones," said Baxter, popping the top of one of the brown bottles. "A Baxter's Beatnik Brews original."

Besides being a freelance journalist who wrote for several publications in the area, Baxter James was the brewmaster and owner of what was locally known as B-Cubed.

"Just so long as it doesn't have wintergreen in it," Ben said with a shudder. "That was a *big* mistake."

"I'll say," Kendra said under her breath. "Couldn't give that shit away, and I bought two full kegs of it."

"Hey, now, come on," said Baxter, playing hurt. "A brewmaster can't come up with a winner every time. And I was trying to make it very, you know, Up North in Michigan."

"Oh, man, that's *good*," Ben said after his first sip. Then he went back in for a second, larger taste (he'd learned from experience not to take a big slug of any "test" B-Cubed beers). "Oh, that's *really* good, Baxter." He looked at Kendra. "I need something to eat with this...maybe some nachos? Heavy on the chili and jalapeños. Extra sour cream."

"You got it," she said. "Bax? You want anything?"

"Make it two. I think you're right," said the brewmaster. "Nachos and maple sugar stout—a match made in heaven. Hey, Dec. You made it!"

Ben turned to see Declan Zyler[1], a blacksmith who'd recently moved back to Wicks Hollow in order to raise his teenaged daughter when her mother moved out east. Apparently, Dec hadn't even known he had a kid until the daughter called him out of the blue about two years ago.

"I heard there was free beer," Dec said, slapping Ben on the back as he slid onto the next stool. "Good to see you, Ben. So glad the Trivia King is here—I hope you're going to stick around. Oh, hey, I promise I'll get those end of year numbers to you tomorrow, all right? Sorry about the delay. I hate doing that sort of stuff."

Ben nodded. "No worries. I can't believe Steph let you out of the house."

They all laughed because Stephanie, Declan's daughter, was now sixteen and had her driver's license. Which meant she was *never* home—at least according to Declan. And her new-found freedom was, according to Declan, the cause of a lot of silvery gray popping up in his dark auburn hair.

"She and Leslie went up to Grand Rapids for a concert. Barry Manilow of all things. Hey, what are we drinking?" Declan picked up one of the unlabeled bottles and gave Baxter a hopeful look.

"Yeah, give it a try."

"So Trib says Callie's in town," said Kendra, giving Ben a knowing look as she set an empty plate and napkin-wrapped flatware in front of him.

Crap. Trust Kendra to remember his crush on Callie from all those years ago. She'd even helped him make a Valentine's Day card for Callie when he was in fifth grade and it wasn't cool for guys to like girls. He'd given it to her anonymously, of course, and he didn't think she ever knew who it came from.

"Yeah. I just saw her over at the clock tower," he replied, keeping his voice very casual. He hoped the slight flush he felt creeping over his face wasn't noticeable. At least the beard would help.

"The old creepy, cursed place?" said Baxter. "What was she doing there?"

"She's getting married there—get this—on New Year's Eve," Ben told him, avoiding Kendra's eyes. But he still felt the weight of them as they locked on him.

"On New Year's Eve? Are you serious?" Baxter swiveled on his stool to look at him. "That's...brave."

"Why is that brave?" asked Declan, sampling the beer. "Oh, yes, this is *so* much better than that wildflower honey wheat beer you tried before. I think I need a veggie omelette to go with it, Kendra."

"How about nachos instead?" she replied. "Eggs and beer...no way. Not in my bar."

"Uh, sure?" Declan glanced at Ben and Baxter, both of whom shrugged. "If you don't want to serve eggs and beer, why do you have omelettes on the menu?"

She shook her head as she wiped up the thickly shellacked counter. "Because Andy makes the best omelettes in the county, that's why. You just can't have one with beer."

Declan gave her a confused look, then shrugged. "All right, now that we have that settled...who is Callie by the way?"

"Callie Quigley," said Kendra, still, apparently, feeling the need to be nosy and interfering, "is Ben's big crush from—when was it—first grade?—all the way through senior year of high school. He made her the sweetest pink and purple valentine when he was in fifth grade. He even put butterflies on it because she had these cute butterfly ponytail holders she used to wear all the time."

Ben took another swig of beer. He should have just gone back to the office, dammit. "Well, I thought they were really cute," he said when Baxter and Declan looked at him. "The butterfly things in her hair."

"She was cute. Is probably still cute. But he was too shy to tell her—ten years of crushing on her from a distance, you know—and then he graduated and went off to college and that was the end of that." Kendra gave him a sympathetic look that was just about to fray his last nerve.

Just then, rescue came along in the form of the Trivia Night emcee pushing through the door. He was toting all of his equipment and that caused enough distraction for Kendra that she left the three guys alone to eat their nachos and drink the beer.

Thank goodness. Ben didn't need anymore reason to be thinking about Callie Quigley.

But when, a few hours later, he caught a glimpse of her bright hair as she walked by The Roost, his heart gave a sad little tug.

You missed your chance, dude.

---

1. *Sinister Secrets*

CHAPTER 3

"SO YOUR BIG marketing idea is to have a wedding at the same place and time as five other weddings that ended with someone dying?" Fiona Murphy looked at Callie with a raised brow. "Like, you're going to be *challenging* a curse?"

They were sitting at a corner table in Orbra's Tea House, which was decked out for the holidays in reds, greens, and blues. Ornate Christmas bulbs hung from ribbons at the windows, a small poinsettia surrounded by candles sat in the center of each table, and the place settings were all in red, green, or gold (patrons could get blue and white for Hanukkah by request).

Orbra used only Christmas or winter-themed tea sets during the month of December, when the menu featured her Holiday Tea specials—which included, among other treats, miniature gingerbread houses, raspberry filled snowball puffs, and apricot-sized pies with savory herb stuffing and a dollop of cranberry sauce. She even did peppermint petit fours with red fondant and minuscule candy canes on them.

"Well, when you put it like that...yes," Callie replied with a grin...which faded after a minute. The heaviness and twisting hadn't left the pit of her stomach since last night.

Maybe she *was* making a mistake.

"I mean, I just assumed that this curse thing was a bunch of exaggerated old tall tales that people piled on over the last, you know, century. But then I went over there yesterday, and..." Callie huffed out a nervous breath. "There's definitely still some strange vibes over there."

"What do you mean *still*?" Fiona asked, placing tiny raspberry-filled snowballs on her small plate. They sparkled from the coarse sugar that coated their outsides.

"Well, the last time I was there—the only time I was there, really—was sixteen years ago. A bunch of us decided to celebrate New Year's Eve in the Tremaine Tower room to prove that there wasn't any curse—and so we could drink and smoke without our parents knowing. It was Ben Tremaine, and—"

"Ben Tremaine, the accountant?" Fiona's eyes suddenly went wide. "Oh, crap, I forgot...I've got to get him my end of year projections!" She groaned and glanced out the front window of the cafe as if expecting to see Ben standing there, watching her expectantly.

Fiona had recently inherited the old antiques shop on Violet Way in Wicks Hollow[1], which was how Callie had met her. It was during a visit last summer and Callie had been looking for some vintage or antique plates for one of the weddings she was planning, and the two had hit it off quite well. Callie ended up buying three sets of Art Deco candlesticks and a large serving platter and making a close friend in the process.

"Yes, that's Ben, I guess. Does he do *everyone's* taxes here in Wicks Hollow?" Callie asked, feeling a stab of pride for her old friend.

She could feel that for him, couldn't she? Just as a friend and not a love interest—even though he'd basically blown her off last night?

Maybe he really *had* had work to do.

"Anyway, it was Ben and me, and Frida Acerita—you know, Juanita's baby sister's daughter—and Randy Johnston, Lauren Barclay, Freddie Cooper, and...oh, what was his name? I can't remember. We were the nerdy kids that hung out and played D&D, PlayStation—*never* XBox—and Settlers of Catan all the time instead of going to sporting events or proms. Anyway, we were all going to hang out and play Spin the Bottle Truth or Dare, and listen to music and smoke and drink and just have a great time ringing in the new year—and none of us were afraid of any curse."

Fiona's lips twitched. "Let me guess. Something very weird happened."

"Yep. It was almost midnight, and we'd been sitting around and had finished about three bottles of Asti between us—plus we'd passed around the bong a few times," she said with a little bit of a wince. "Anyway, as you can imagine, we were all feeling pretty loose and really confident. 'Look at this. It's five minutes to midnight! No curse is going to scare *us* out of here,' said Freddie. I remember that because about a minute later, I was—uh, Ben and I were—uh..." *Damn.* Callie felt her face go hot and she knew how bright the blush would be over her dead-white skin.

"You and Ben were...?" Fiona said teasingly.

"Well, we happened to end up standing under the mistletoe that Frida hung up because *she* wanted to catch

Randy under it, but he was only interested in Lauren—I think, anyway—and anyway...Ben and I were standing there and suddenly Frida shouts, 'Oooh! Callie, look up! You're under the mistletoe! Ben, you're the closest one—give her a kiss!'" Callie couldn't believe that sixteen years later, she was *still* blushing over that moment.

Fiona was watching her from over the rim of her crimson teacup. Her lips curved in a delighted smile behind the cup's gold-painted rim. "Well, did he?"

"He sure did." Callie couldn't quite keep the zest from her voice, and her face went even hotter when she realized how she sounded. "I mean..."

"Happy New Year to you, huh?" giggled Fiona. "So... what happened?"

"Well, we were—uh—kissing, you know—"

"So it wasn't just an obligatory peck on the cheek," Fiona said, still grinning.

"Um. *No.* Definitely not just a peck on the cheek." Callie figured her face was so hot it would light up the entire city if she were outside at night right now. Geez. How mortifying. She was a grown woman, many years and several relationships past that night...why did she still react so strongly to the memory?

"So, anyway, you and Ben were mauling each other—what do they say in England? Oh, yes, *snogging* under the mistletoe, and some asshole guy has to tempt fate by saying, 'See, there's no ghosts here,' or whatever..."

Callie nodded, laughing. "Yeah. That was about it. The next thing I knew, the entire room was...well, it was like we were in a tornado or a crazy windstorm or something. Everything just sort of erupted." She shivered, and felt a little sick to her stomach as she remembered the way they stumbled and fought to try and find their way out of the room. "We couldn't see where we were going; it was kind of dark and we only had two small flashlights—and they went out right away.

"Everyone was totally freaked out and we were shouting and bumping into each other, and then one of us—I think it was Lauren, or maybe it was the guy whose name I can't remember—oh, Darren, that's it—opened the door and we started to run out but it was the wrong door and suddenly we were out on the balcony where all those people had died on New Year's Eve—"

She shook her head, remembering the wild terror that coursed through her. *People had died there!*

"The clock was chiming midnight and the ball was going to light up on the twelfth stroke, and the next thing I knew Ben was grabbing me and dragging me and Lauren back inside, saying, 'Get off there! Get back inside!' and finally all of us were back in the room, which was still crazy wild...and then it felt like it was raining *inside*—there was all this wet stuff flinging around. We somehow got out the right door and ran down the stairs and..." She spread her hands. Her heart was pounding hard, as if she were living the horror all over again. "When we got downstairs and outside and got a look at each other...we were all covered in specks and droplets of—of blood. I mean, it looked like blood. Like it had been splattered all over us."

She shivered, feeling the same ugly nausea she'd experienced that night when she looked at her friends and their terrified, blood-splattered faces.

"That really freaked us out, and we just—ran away. Went home. It took me a long time to wash whatever that was off my face. I don't know if it was blood, but whatever it was..." She shuddered. "I don't think any of us wanted to talk about what happened or to admit it...and we didn't really hang out together much after that. For the same reason. It was...crazy."

"And so after living through all of that, you decided it was a good idea to have a wedding there on New Year's Eve?" Fiona asked.

Callie sighed and bit her lip. "It was so long ago, and I never heard of anyone else having any sort of experience there. I think over the years I sort of talked myself into believing that one of the guys had set it up to freak us all out—and that we were so drunk and stoned that we exaggerated all of it. You know?" She picked up one of the miniature gingerbread houses—the size of a large muffin—its features painstakingly piped with frosting. She bit off the chimney with a sharp snap. "But after being there yesterday..." She shivered. "Maybe I was wrong."

"Can I just point out that this is, after all, Wicks Hollow," said Fiona mildly. "And that kind of stuff is *real* here."

"Well, that's one of the reasons I wanted to talk to you about it. Because...didn't *you* have a ghost problem or some-thing? In your shop?"

"I certainly did. And, fortunately, it's been resolved." Fiona poured a new cup of tea for each of them. "The ghost—whose name was Gretchen, by the way, has been happily put to rest."

Callie inhaled the delicious scent of a vanilla spice oolong that was Orbra's signature blend for her Holiday Teas. Mmmm. Delicious. "Well, that's the thing—maybe if we can resolve—I mean, if *I* can resolve whatever is going on with that place before New Year's Eve, then it'll be safe for Iva and Hollis to get married there."

"*What?*" Fiona's cup clattered onto its saucer, sloshing tea all over the table. "*Who?*"

"Oh, it's this darling older couple who are just gaga over each other. The groom is an old friend of Mom's second husband, and—"

"Are you talking about Iva Bergstrom and Hollis Nath?" Fiona's eyes were bugging out.

"Yes! Do you know them? Oh, that's right—I think they did mention Iva has a house here. Aren't they the cutest—"

"Callie, you can't do that! You can't—wait, wait, *wait...* how on earth did you get Iva to agree to *that*? She's got *serious* respect for ghosts and the supernatural...I can't see her ever agreeing to—I don't know—disrupting a curse of whatever by doing something that's like—like poking a bear!"

Callie was a little taken aback by Fiona's ferocity. She wasn't offended, she was just surprised. But maybe someone who'd dealt with her own ghostly situation wasn't about to play fast and loose with another one.

And maybe Fiona was correct about that...

"Right. Well, actually, I don't think Mr. Nath has told Iva about the actual venue yet. I think it was going to be a surprise...?" The expression on Fiona's face had Callie grimacing in defeat. "Not good?"

Fiona was shaking her head. "I don't know whether to laugh or cry. Poor Hollis. He's going to get himself in a crapton of trouble once Iva finds out he volunteered them for this crazy publicity stunt—that's what it is, right? And how did that end up happening anyway?"

Callie was feeling utterly miserable by this point. "Well, I was trying to find a way to bolster my off-season wedding planning services, and so I decided it would be fun to offer free wedding planning and vendor services to whatever couple was willing to tie the knot on the Tremaine Tower balcony on New Year's Eve. Kind of like a curse-debunking contest sort of thing.

"Mr. Nath heard about it through my mom, and he jumped on the chance—I think because he's ready to tie the knot and it sounds like Iva's been in not so much of a rush. Not because he can't afford it, of course, but because I guess once Iva said she thought it would be the most romantic thing in the world to get married in the snow, outside on New Year's Eve.

"So Mr. Nath thought he'd kill two birds with one stone —do a favor for the daughter of a friend, me, and present his bride with her dream wedding."

Fiona was shaking her head. "Oh boy. It'll be a miracle if they *ever* get married once Iva finds out about this. Have you ever met a woman who *didn't* want to be in charge of planning her own wedding?"

"Oh, that's not a problem—the reason Mr. Nath wanted to do it is because I was already meeting with them to discuss doing their wedding anyway. That's how I know how ridiculously adorable the two of them are. I got enough information from Iva to know what she likes and what she'd want—and apparently, she agreed that Mr. Nath could pick the venue as long as it's on New Year's Eve. So he's making it a sort of surprise."

"It'll be a surprise all right," Fiona muttered. "All right. So. Assuming Iva doesn't murder Hollis when she finds out about his master plan, and the wedding is going to go on as scheduled...you're going to need to figure out how to put this curse—and its ghost—to rest. Right?"

"Right." Callie heaved a sigh of relief that she'd got Fiona back on her side. "But how do I do that?"

Fiona settled back in her seat. "Well, you could do what Leslie Nakano did up at Shenstone House when she was being haunted—actually try and talk to the ghost and see what she—or he, or whatever—will tell you."

"I was already planning to do some serious research about Brenda Tremaine—yes, she's some relation to Ben; that's how we got access to the building back then because they still own the place—and the others who died. I guess that's where I should start."

"Yes. And you'd better get on it pretty soon, since New Year's Eve is only three weeks from tomorrow," Fiona said, baring her teeth in a humorless smile. Then her expression turned crafty. "Why don't you ask cutie Ben Tremaine to help you do the research. He's still single, you know, and it's his own family's building. And I do like his beard."

"I do too," Callie said. And blushed.

Dammit.

---

1. *Sinister Shadows.*

CHAPTER 4

DECEMBER WAS the busiest time of the year for most people, but when you were an event planner—especially one who specialized in weddings—the craziness was off the charts. Thus Callie had Christmas-themed weddings, *Nutcracker* premieres, and holiday parties up the wazoo.

That was why it was a whole week later before Callie had time to make the ninety-minute drive to Wicks Hollow from her home base in Grand Rapids.

T-minus fourteen days till the Crazy Cursed Tremaine Tower Wedding.

Why am I doing this to myself?

The problem was, it was too late to change things now. Not only had she promised a gorgeous wedding event for Iva Bergstrom and Hollis Nath, but she'd booked (and paid for, nonrefundably) the photographer, musicians, invitations, flowers, and food...and aside from *that*, she'd had five "teaser" pieces in various midwest publications about the Breaking of the Tremaine Clock Tower Curse wedding.

She'd been on the local television morning show in Grand Rapids, and had been interviewed on two different radio stations. Numerous blogs—both wedding planner-type blogs and ghost-hunter blogs—had picked up the story and reposted it.

Even Baxter James, the cute and shy brewmaster who did freelance writing for some of the local papers, had done a big spread for the *Grand Rapids Press*—complete with photos of not only Callie and her office, but also Hollis Nath (who was a bigwig lawyer in the city and seemed to know everyone) and his bride...along with photos from the fateful night Brenda and Barclay had tried to get married.

In short, she'd trumpeted her intentions far and wide via as many avenues as possible, so now *everyone* (or at least it felt like everyone) knew about the wedding that was meant to break a deadly curse.

What was I thinking?

But pulling out now or changing venues would leave an ugly stain on her business and leave Callie looking like an irresponsible and unreliable wedding planner.

She sighed and tuned in the radio to a satellite All Christmas All The Time station as she sped along the highway. Thank goodness the snow that had been promised wasn't supposed to hit for at least another three hours. She might not get to Wicks Hollow and the Tremaine Tower until the sun was just setting, but at least she wouldn't be driving in a lake effect snowstorm.

It was Tuesday—the only night she really had free between now and December 27th—and it was the last chance she'd have to look at the Bergstrom/Nath venue before it was crunch time. Every other evening between now and then was busy with holiday parties and weddings—not to mention Christmas itself—and the days were filled with last-minute meetings, decoration finalizations, and food tastings.

Fortunately, most of the parties she had going on were with regular vendors and venues, so even though CQEvents never took any party for granted, at least she knew the gigs and their settings very well and was comfortable with each of them.

Except for the Bergstrom/Nath wedding. That was definitely a growing concern, potential curse notwithstanding.

Callie had sent a list of requests to the caretaker related to getting lights fixed and checking on the stability of the stairs and balcony. The Tremaines had agreed she could replace the curtains in the anteroom, so Callie had put a rush on those. She'd also hired a cleaning crew to go in and clean out the antechamber and sweep up the spiral stairs, so at least that should be in better shape than last time.

The mistletoe would surely be gone.

But so would all the critters, she hoped.

Callie still had the building key from before, so she didn't expect to run into anyone, like the caretaker—even though she'd sent a last-minute email that she would be checking the venue tonight. There was no chance she'd run into Ben Tremaine.

Which was good, because when she left to go home last week, she'd walked by the Roost on the way to her car. And she was pretty sure she'd seen him in there, sitting with a bunch of guys. They looked like they were playing Trivia, and whoever they were, they'd be lucky to have him on their team. The guy knew everything.

But apparently he hadn't been that busy after all.

Callie had too much to do to spend any time feeling awkward or shy around him anyway. He'd be far too busy doing end of year numbers for—it seemed—half of the businesses in Wicks Hollow, to be checking up on her anyway.

Callie parked on the street not far from Trib's, which was packed to the gills even though it was a Tuesday night in the off-season. It looked like standing room only from her viewpoint as she climbed out of her car. No surprise. Her uncle's restaurant was known throughout the county as the trendiest, most fabulous eatery, and it was booked for business dinners, client thank you dinners, and family dinners from the day after Thanksgiving through New Year's Day. Despite being his niece—and Iva Bergstrom being his good friend—Callie considered herself lucky that Trib's had actually agreed to cater the New Year's Eve wedding.

As she walked down the street toward the tower, whose illuminated clock face indicated it was after four-thirty, she passed a street-level door squashed between Gilda's Goodies and Dek Home Designs. The sign on the door leaped out at her: *Tremaine & Associates. Benjamin D. Tremaine, CPA.*

She glanced through the door's window as she walked past and saw the flight of stairs that led to what must be his second-floor office space. And then she looked up to see that the lights were on. Being on the sidewalk below, she was too close to the side of the building to see much more than that, but for some reason, it made her smile knowing that Ben had done so well for himself.

The air was crisp and cold, and she could smell the snow that was coming. She might have to crash at Uncle Trib's instead of driving all the way back to Grand Rapids tonight, if the storm was as bad as the reports suggested. Even as she crossed the small square and strode past the towering pine decorated in silver and gold, large, puffy flakes began to drift down from an iron gray sky.

The tower looked like a lonely gray stub beneath its glowing face, but as Callie drew near, she saw signs that progress had been made. The walkway was shoveled and a wreath had been hung on the door. And when she unlocked the exterior door and stepped inside, she immediately noticed the difference.

The place smelled fresh, and the debris that had been there last week had been swept away.

Progress.

Callie climbed up the steps, feeling better about things already. Maybe whatever weirdness she'd experienced the other day had been swept away, cleaned out, or otherwise banished as well.

The key worked more easily in the lock this time—it had probably been oiled.

When she stepped inside the room, the first thing she noticed was that it was completely empty. The old chairs, table, dusty and broken bottles—and, yes, the mistletoe—were all gone. The floor was clean and she could smell the faint hint of whatever wood polish had been used there and on the mahogany wainscoting around the room.

The portrait of Brenda Tremaine had been replaced on the wall. Callie eyed it a little nervously as she felt around for the light switch that, at her request, had been fixed and should now be working.

She pushed the old-fashioned light switch button and soft yellow light from six century-old sconces filled the room.

The floor had the dull sheen of having recently been cleaned, and even the windows sparkled.

All at once she felt more optimistic than she'd been in a while. The wedding itself would take place out on the balcony at midnight, and the guests would be on the ground below, watching as the happy couple exchanged vows just before the clock struck twelve.

The bells would ring and the ball would light up. There would be beautiful photo ops for the glowing couple—she hoped for just a little bit of wafting snow—and then they'd all come inside the small anteroom for *hors d'oeuvres* and celebration. A string trio would provide suitable background music.

"Well," Callie said aloud, "I hope you don't mind your—uh—new digs. So to speak." For some reason, she didn't feel weird talking to the portrait of the ill-fated Brenda Tremaine. "Maybe it'll make you more..."

She didn't finish the sentence because the air had started to swirl again. The curtains, which had already been replaced from the moth-eaten ones by dark green velvet, were too heavy to buffet in the air, but the fringe on the tie-backs shimmied.

The environment became frigid so quickly she actually gasped, drawing in a knife-sharp cold into her nostrils. Then she huffed out a breath that literally turned into ice crystals the minute the droplets hit the air. Her nose felt as if it would break off if she rubbed it, and though she thrust her hands deep in her pockets and curled them inside their gloves, it felt as though her fingers were submerged in ice water. It was painful to breathe the arctic air.

"Oh, come on..." Callie said, turning in a slow circle as

she looked around the room. "No one's trying to—to disrespect you, Brenda. It's been nearly a century...couldn't you just—"

Whoosh!

The gust of wind came from nowhere and began to whip at the hem of her coat with startling violence. Her hat went flying and suddenly the air was filled with dust or dirt or something that obstructed her view so that she was in a tornado of darkness.

"Noooooooo."

Callie didn't know where the voice came from, but it filled her ears as if it were being pumped through great speakers all around the room.

"Nooooooo.

"Nooooooo!"

The cry was something not quite human, not quite real, and it filled her, reverberating through her body in a violent shudder.

Callie was paralyzed with shock and terror. She felt wetness on her face and realized she was sobbing as the wind and some tiny hard *things* pelted her unforgivingly. She stumbled around, trying to find her way out of the storm, and finally her hand brushed the wall. Using it for stability, she felt her way along, seeking the door, as she was battered and buffeted by Brenda Tremaine's wrath.

Then from somewhere, she heard bells ringing—a deep tolling that cut through the wild maelstrom around her. And suddenly, the tornado winds ceased and the pelting stopped... and Callie was once again standing in the soft glow of yellow light.

All was quiet and still except for the last toll of bells striking the hour of five.

Shaking, still sobbing a little, Callie dragged a hand across her face to wipe away the tears.

Brenda Tremaine had definitely made her opinion clear.

Now what was Callie going to do?

CHAPTER 5

BEN WAS JUST LOCKING the street-level door to his office when he heard a sound like a frustrated cry, followed by a dull thud-like clunk—like someone had kicked something metal. Possibly the side of a car.

He looked around, and to his shock and amazement saw Callie Quigley standing on the sidewalk glowering at a car parked on the street. Presumably hers.

The wind had begun to pick up and the sleety, thick snow that had been forecast was falling with a vengeance—hence the reason he was heading home at just after five o'clock. He could work there in front of the fireplace with a glass of wine and not have to worry about digging out his car to drive home at eight or nine.

"Callie? Is that you? Everything okay?" he asked, tugging the hat down over his head and huddling against the blizzard.

"Oh, Ben," she said, and when she turned her face to look at him he gasped.

"What happened to you?" He didn't even think about

what he was doing when he took her by the chin to look at her face. "Are you all right?"

She looked at him funny, then pulled her chin away—not like she was mad he'd touched her, thank goodness, but because she seemed confused. "Well, no, I'm not, but—"

"What's all over your face?"

"My face?" She reached up with a gloved hand to touch her cheek, which was pink with cold but also speckled with dark red streaks.

"It looks like—like blood or something. Are you hurt?" He was shaken, just looking at her with all those ugly streaks on her face.

"I—oh my God, really?" Horrified, she put her hands to her face and began to scrub at it. Her eyes were wide and terrorized. "It was her. Oh my God, it had to be her! That's what all the wetness was!"

"Her who?" Every one of Ben's instincts screamed at him to pull her close and hold her—or to bundle her into his car and drive her to the emergency room. He did neither— though it was supremely difficult—and instead simply reached over to brush away some of the wild snowflakes that had fallen onto her cheeks.

"Brenda Tremaine." She dropped her hands from her face and looked up at him.

Under the streetlamp, her eyes were wide and impossibly, beautifully blue. The bluster of snow swirled around, landing on the tips of her coppery eyelashes and nose, scattering among the splash of girlish freckles that still brushed her cheeks and forehead at the age of thirty-two. Despite the horrifying splatters of blood—or whatever it was—on her nose and chin, Callie looked simply beautiful: glowing and soft and just so feminine. Her lips were full and puffy and pink, and when a cluster of snowflakes landed on the upper one, it was all he could do to keep from kissing it away.

Then her words sunk in. "Brenda Tremaine?" he repeated, then stopped. "Let's back up. First, are you hurt?"

"No. I'm—"

"Just...one thing at a time, all right?" he said, holding up his hands to slow her down. "There's a lot going on here...like, why are you kicking your car?"

"I can't find my keys. I think—I think they're back there." She thumbed toward the village square, and he realized she meant the Clock Tower. "I think they must have fallen out of my pocket during...during..." Her voice suddenly seemed to stop working and she looked up at him wordlessly.

Now he could see tears filling her eyes and that the tip of her nose was turning even darker pink.

"All right. All right. It's all right. You're okay now, right?"

She nodded, and he put an arm around her. He allowed himself to give her a brief squeeze, then prudently let go. "How about...what do you think about getting out of this blizzard and settling down for a—a drink or something, and you can tell me about what happened. But first...how about if I go over and see if I can find your keys? If you dropped them in the snow—"

"I didn't drop them outside. I'm s-sure it was in the room up there, when Brenda kind of went ballistic at me. Like what h-happened before, you know?"

He understood that she meant what happened sixteen years ago, not last week. "All right. I'll go over and see if I can find them—you think you dropped them in the room?"

"I didn't *drop* them—I think they must have fallen out of

my pocket. But I'm going with you! I was just about to go back over there when you came out. I was just so *mad* that I got all the way here and realized I didn't have my keys. I'm not afraid to go back there," she added defensively.

"No, of course not," he said, wondering if he would be saying the same if it had happened to him. "Come on, I'll go with you. We'll find your keys, and then you can be on your way back home."

To your fiancé.

Ben gritted his teeth and was glad he hadn't indulged himself in more than a brief hug.

They were nearly to the edge of the square when suddenly Callie stopped short. "Ohmi*god*," she said. She sounded furious.

All at once she was unzipping her coat—there in the middle of the blizzard—and moments later she produced a jangling keyring from deep inside. "I forgot that I put them in the inside pocket because I had to have my phone and my flashlight in my other pockets, and I didn't want the keys to fall out when I took out my flash—never mind. Ugh. I never do that—put my keys or anything inside there. I have no idea why I decided to do it this time. Sorry, Ben. That's what happens when you've got too many things on your mind and too many balls in the air and a freaking *ghost* is trying t-to ruin everything." Her voice wavered, but she managed to get all the words out.

"All right, then, that's good that you found them," Ben said. He guessed that meant she'd be climbing in her car and driving away in a few minutes.

Which was just as well. Really.

The less temptation the better.

"So," she said, having turned an about-face and was heading back toward where her car had been parked. "What were you saying about a drink?"

She beamed up at him as they walked, and despite all the blood-red streaks on her face, she looked much happier than a moment ago.

"Um...well, sure, of course. I don't suppose we could get a table at Trib's right now—"

"Not a chance. Besides, I can't really go in there looking like Carrie at the prom, you know," she said, gesturing to herself. "That would give Uncle Trib a heart attack. Isn't your office nearby?"

"Oh, yeah, it is, but I don't really have anything there to offer you—I mean, besides coffee or tea or bottled water. There might be a can of soda or some granola bars."

"Oh."

"But I've got some wine and beer at my house—it's not far from here," he said before he could stop himself. "You could get cleaned up there, you know, and—"

"Do you have a printer there?" she jumped in.

"Yes, of course."

"Oh, that would be perfect. I've got to print off something and I was going to stop at Uncle Trib's office and do it, but I don't want to bother him. The restaurant looks like it's bursting at the seams."

And that was how Callie ended up at Ben's house.

Which was really not a good idea.

But at the same time, it was the *best* idea.

She followed him in her car the half mile out of the central area of town to the neat, white clapboard Cape Cod that was barely two blocks from the Lake Michigan shore.

As Ben unlocked the front door and stepped back to let her in, he did a quick mental and visual inventory as to what condition he'd left the place this morning. To his relief, the only disarray was his coffee cup and cereal bowl in the sink, and a laundry basket with clean clothes that he'd neglected to take back to the bedroom.

"Oh, Ben, that is so *you*," Callie said as she dumped her coat, handbag, and what looked like a briefcase on the nearest sofa and headed straight for his six-foot-tall fresh pine Christmas tree.

"What do you mean?"

She turned back to him, still wearing her soft, fuzzy blue hat. Tilting her head, she gave him such a sweet, affectionate smile that he nearly melted right there. "Well, it's all color-coordinated, and the bulbs are all matching and spaced perfectly. It's very organized. It's just so *you*. And I love the *Avengers* ornament."

She was beaming at him and although Ben didn't know what was so funny, he didn't mind because she was so darn pretty, and she was looking at him with those fathomless blue eyes—

And he was going to be in deep trouble if he wasn't careful.

"Thanks. I really like having a real tree instead of a fake one, even though it starts to drop needles after a week," he replied, trying to keep things casual. "So, uh, if you want to wash up, there's the bathroom right down that hall."

She disappeared into the bathroom while he hung up his coat, and no sooner had she closed the door than she shrieked.

"Callie? What is it?" He started down the hall, wondering if he was going to have to break into the bathroom.

"Oh, sorry," she called back. "Oh, it's nothing. I just saw what I looked like. Um. *Yikes.*" Her voice sounded awkward from the other side of the door, and he heard the splash of water.

"Okay. Uh, there are towels in the closet there."

Ben finished hanging up his coat, and then because he didn't know what to do next, and it was a structured, soothing task, he started stacking wood in the fireplace.

The blaze was roaring happily by the time Callie came out, her face damp and shining and little red—probably from all the scrubbing. He remembered how difficult it had been to get that red stuff off his face and hands sixteen years ago. To his surprise, she was still wearing her hat.

"Wow," she said. "A real fire—not one of those gas ones."

"Yeah. I could have put in a gas insert, but I decided I didn't mind the extra work of cleaning out the ashes and chopping and hauling in the wood. It's good exercise, you know?"

"So you chop all your own wood?" She lifted one brow and eyed him thoughtfully. "I bet that *is* good exercise. A really good workout for the biceps too, huh?"

Ben nearly swallowed his tongue. Was she *flirting* with him?

Of course not.

She was getting married in two weeks.

"Um, I hung up your coat—did you want to put your hat with it?"

"Oh, no, that's all right." She reached up to touch the

pom-pom hanging down the back of it, but didn't remove the hat.

He shrugged, but didn't press. "So, what would you like to drink? And do you want something to eat? It's about dinner time. For me at least."

"A glass of wine would be nice. Whatever you have open is fine. I could definitely eat, but please don't go to any trouble—do you maybe have a frozen pizza or something?"

She was wandering around looking at the books on his shelf in the living room, pausing at the photographs of his family—which included those from the fly fishing trips he took every year with his dad, grandfather, brothers, and nephews—as well as a few wedding pictures from his siblings.

Ben realized he felt a little tense about what she might think of him having all sorts of boring family pictures everywhere, but no artwork or anything interesting on the walls or table...except old copies of *American Angler* and *Sport Fishing*.

"I have some frozen beef stew," he said. "And fresh sourdough bread from my buddy Jake DeRiccio. I can put the stew in the oven to warm, which will take a while, and then I think you'd better tell me about Brenda Tremaine."

"Ugh." Callie heaved a great sigh and plumped down on the sofa in front of the fireplace. "This is really nice. Do we have to ruin it?" She gave him a wistful smile, then shook her head. "Of course we do. I'm really grateful you're willing to listen."

He'd be happy to do a lot more than listen, but that ship had sailed. Dammit. When he brought her a glass of Cabernet (he'd opened a new bottle because the one he'd had a few nights ago was just about to turn and he didn't want to ruin the evening with bad wine), she took it with pleasure.

He hesitated for a minute, then ended up sitting at the other end of the sofa instead of the armchair. He told himself it was because that seat was closer to the kitchen and the fire-place, but he was lying. It was closer to Callie, and that was all that mattered.

"So I'm in deep trouble, Ben," she said right away.

"All right," he replied cautiously.

She looked down into her glass, swirling the dark red wine into such an enthusiastic vortex that he half expected it to slosh out all over her and the sofa. He smiled deep inside—that was Callie. She rarely did anything halfway.

"Brenda Tremaine has made it abundantly clear she is *not* going to allow a wedding," Callie said. "I tried to talk to her today and she just freaked out. You saw me—I don't know what that red stuff was all over me, but it wasn't confetti. She's mad and she's not going to back down." She grimaced and took another sip of wine, then tilted her head onto the back of the couch.

This left her throat bare—a gentle, arc of pale skin above the modest vee-neck of the fuzzy sweater she was wearing. Perfect—just perfect—to drop a soft kiss on, right there in the hollow of her throat...and follow along that warm, sensitive line up to her chin and below her ear...

Ben swallowed hard and looked away. "Well, can't you just move your wedding to a different place?"

Or cancel it all together?

She huffed a sigh as she lifted her head back up. "I mean, of course I can. But I chose that venue *because* of the Clock Tower Curse—it's a publicity-slash-marketing sort of thing, you know?" She shifted in her seat, moving back into the corner of the couch and bringing up one foot to tuck under her as she turned to face him. "And, dammit, it's not right that Brenda Tremaine—who died ninety-some years ago—is holding your family's tower hostage! I mean, I know she died, I know it was a tragedy, but she needs to get over it and let life for us mortals go on!"

"Well, yes, I suppose you're right. But Brenda wasn't the only person to die there—how do you know it's her that's—uh—holding the place hostage, as you say? And I can't even believe I'm *saying* this." He gave a short laugh and shook his head. "It's wild."

"It's Wicks Hollow," Callie told him.

"I guess."

"And anyway, I know it's her because I was talking to her portrait and I addressed her. I figured—well, I don't know, I thought if I just acknowledged her as a ghost, she might..." She exhaled violently. "This is crazy talk. I know. And yet..."

"It's Wicks Hollow." He lifted his glass in a mock toast and they both laughed.

When his eyes lit up with humor and his mouth tipped up behind his beard and mustache, Callie *really* wanted to lunge down the sofa toward him and smack a kiss on his cheek. But she hadn't gotten any sort of vibe from him that he would appreciate or reciprocate such a move, and so she kept her butt planted right there on the couch.

"The way I look at it is, I've got three choices. One, cancel the wedding—or at least the venue, which I really *really* don't want to do. Two, do it anyway, and just let the chips fall where they may—"

"But someone might die," Ben interjected.

"I know. I *know*. I don't want anyone to die, that's for sure." She huffed again. "Or, my third option is to try and figure out how to put Brenda Tremaine's ghost to rest so we *can* have the wedding there.

"It's just going to be so beautiful, Ben! We're going to do a forest of white painted trees on the balcony, sprayed with glitter paint. They're not really trees, but big branches that just look like trees," she added when he gave her a skeptical look. "And the balcony railing itself is going to be swagged with greenery and lights with a big wreath hanging from the center, right where the pictures will all be taken. It'll be at midnight, of course, and so we're actually going to do about three dozen hurricanes all over the balcony—"

"Hurricanes?" He looked very confused.

"Oh, you know, glass containers with candles in them to protect from the wind. All different sizes and shapes, and all the candles will be in cream or ecru or champagne colors. And some of them will hold three candles, some only two or one...it's going to look so stunningly beautiful." She sighed.

She'd never done an outdoor winter wedding before—after all, who did something like that? Well, CQEvents did! She hoped anyway. And if she pulled it off, it was going to be *so* gorgeous.

"And the bride will be wearing an elegant evening suit in ecru, trimmed with big white fur lapels and cuffs, and a lovely fur hat that looks a little like those big Russian things, but prettier."

"Right. Oh, let me check on the stew." Ben popped up from the couch and was gone before Callie could say anything else.

The fire was still raging merrily when, a few moments

later, Ben came back in with a tray of bread and butter, along with two large bowls of stew.

"Wow. This looks great," she said, hardly able to wait to dig in. "Where'd you get the stew?"

"I made it. On the weekend, I like to make big batches of stuff and freeze it so I have an easy dinner during the week."

"You chop your own wood, keep a clean house, and you can cook too? How come no lucky girl's ever snatched you up?" she said, half teasing, half being *very* nosy. And wistful.

Was she imagining it or was he blushing? Good. Maybe that would loosen him up a little.

"Oh, well, I—it just makes sense to plan ahead, you know. Anyway, I was doing some research about the last few weddings on the Tremaine Tower balcony, you know, after last week." He was talking fast, as if trying to change the subject.

So shy and awkward. She just *loved* that about him. He'd always been that way, and that was part of what had attracted her to him, even back in high school when most girls were ga-ga over football or soccer players. But Ben was quiet, steady, intelligent, and calm. And pretty nerdy. Some people might call him boring, but Callie figured she had enough excitement and energy in her personality for the both of them.

"Did you really?" she asked, internally delighted that he'd spent some time worrying about what was really her problem. "Did you find out anything that might help the—uh—situation?"

"I'm not sure. I just wanted to know more about all of the instances. The first one was Brenda and Barclay, of course. Everyone knows about that, and about how Lonna Donne supposedly cursed them and started this unpleasant trend.

That was December 31, 1929. Here's a picture of them right before she collapsed." He tapped on the computer tablet he'd just retrieved and passed it to Callie.

"And they had no idea what caused Brenda to die?" she asked as she looked at the photograph of the beautiful couple.

The bride and groom were holding coupes filled with something that didn't look like champagne—it was a darker color—and they beamed out over the crowd as the leaned over the railing and waved to their friends and family.

Ben shook his head. "No—there wasn't a mark on her, and she didn't have any health problems. No poison or anything like that. I mean, it wasn't like they had CSI in 1930, but they did do postmortems. So the timing of her death and the fact that they couldn't attribute a cause added to the curse story."

Callie had been reading the article and she stopped suddenly. "Oh! *That's* what it is."

"What?" He straightened up in his seat. "You figured it out?"

"Well, I figured out what the red stuff is that was all over my face. I think." She tapped the tablet screen and scrolled to the section in the article. "Brenda and Barclay had had a signature cocktail at their wedding—a cranberry champagne cocktail. She was *holding* a glass of it when she collapsed and died—and the way the newspaper article described her...let me read it to you. 'Her horribly crumpled body lay in a heap of glittering silk, her cocktail glass shattered on the ground beside her. As if to punctuate the terrible moment, there were streaks of red on her face that had splashed up from the drink as Brenda Tremaine collapsed in sudden, inexplicable death.' The journalists were a lot more dramatic in their descriptions back then," she added with a wry smile.

"So she—her ghost—is replicating the moment of her death with the red streaks," Ben said, nodding thoughtfully. "All right, that's logical."

"And cranberry juice really stains," she said. "So what else did you find out about the other deaths?" She handed the tablet back to him.

"All right, so three years later, Peggy Wilmington and Reginald Bowersox decided to have their wedding at Tremaine Tower, and they came out on the balcony to wave to all of their friends when the clock was striking midnight. At the twelfth and final toll of the bells, *both* of them fell to the floor of the balcony—suddenly dead."

"Both of them? How awful." Callie was well into her stew and she was amazed at how good it was. She hoped there was enough for a second helping.

"Right? And same thing—no obvious cause of death was found on either of them. Then no one tried anything until 1939...New Year's Eve, same deal and Felicity Kelly and Patrick McMurtaugh tied the knot in front of a whole lot of their friends and family—some of whom were on the balcony with them. Felicity and Patrick were just about to pose for a picture for a reporter below, and when the clock finished striking midnight and the ball lit up, someone noticed that Felicity had collapsed on the balcony. She was dead as well. No obvious cause of death. So by that time, the idea of the curse had really taken hold, obviously." He paused from scrolling through his tablet to sample the stew for a few bites. "The other two instances—in 1943 and 1947—were similar. And for all of them, there was no clear cause of death. It was like they just dropped dead for no reason. Here, take a look. I pulled up pictures of all of them."

Callie took the tablet again, still feeling moved that he'd spent all this time worrying about her problem. It was his family's building, too, but he didn't seem to have had any interest in the curse until she came along. She smiled to herself. Good old Ben.

She flipped through the photographs he'd pulled into an album, noting the happy couples and their beautiful wedding attire. All were on the balcony, all were above everyone else and waving or looking down at them from the railing. The clock face was above them, and in each of the photos, it was just before midnight.

"The other strange thing is," he said, mopping a crust of bread through the rich brown broth, "there were other events that took place on the balcony over the years. Not many, but there were some...and no one died."

"Hmm. Any weddings?" Callie asked. "I mean, where no one died?"

He shook his head. "No. So they all have that in common."

"And they all took place on New Year's Eve, right around midnight—which is when the first incident took place. So it seems as if the so-called curse only applies to weddings that take place at midnight on New Year's Eve. Great."

"Well, you could always do the wedding earlier than midnight," he said with a sort of pained smile. "Then you might avoid whatever it is that is annoying Brenda Tremaine."

Callie laughed. "That's an option. But, hey, you're a relative of hers—maybe you could talk to her!"

"That would assume I actually know how to talk to ghosts, much less female ghosts," he said, and chuckled. "Which, unless they're clients and talking about deductions and write-offs, I find myself at a loss talking to women. They're just not very interested in fly fishing."

"You've never had trouble talking to me," she said teasingly. "But then the topics of our discussion were all around Dungeons and Dragons and arguing about which Star Trek series is the best." Callie sobered. "Seriously, Ben, why *hasn't* some awesome gal snagged you? Or...is there someone?"

He looked down at his bowl and shrugged. "Not really. There was someone I—uh—had a thing for for a while, but it never went anywhere. But I'm pretty happy with the way things are in my life right now. Though it would be nice to have someone to share this kind of an evening with once in a while." He looked around the room: the fire blazing, the Christmas tree with its perfectly aligned rows of clear, sparkling lights, the comfort food, the overstuffed sofa.

Callie nodded. "This is pretty cozy."

She sighed, tamping back her own twinge of emptiness. She, too, had a fulfilling life with her own exciting business that probably kept her too busy for a relationship anyway. Still, helping so many couples plan their weddings did sometimes make her feel lonely.

She shook herself out of the melancholy and turned a bright—if somewhat forced—smile toward Ben. "Well, I'd better get to that printer if you don't mind. I need to print off a schematic for the florist, and I was going to stick it in her mailbox on my way out of town so they'd have it first thing tomorrow. Margie's not very good with opening email attachments," she added ruefully.

"Oh, yes, I know Margie," Ben replied with a grin. "She gives me a box with her receipts in it every year and refuses to do anything with QuickBooks because it's online."

Callie gave a weak laugh—she was really feeling down in the dumps—and said, "I bet that's a lot of fun! So, where's the printer? I can connect via wifi, right?"

Yes, of course she could connect wirelessly—she was at Ben's house. Callie smiled to herself, but she still felt like crap. It was becoming clearer and clearer to her what she needed to do.

And in doing so, she was going to be letting a lot of people down.

But it was the right thing to do.

CHAPTER 6

WHILE CALLIE WAS PRINTING things off in his home office, Ben took the opportunity to stoke up the fire. He added several logs and by the time she came back into the living room, it was blazing merrily.

He'd turned off the overhead light and the one that beamed in from the kitchen because it seemed so harsh when there was a Christmas tree and a dancing fire to give off a softer light, *not* because he was setting a seduction scene. After all, he'd left the side table lamp on.

But when Callie came out of his office—her hat drooping even more off the back of her head—he took one look at her and knew something was wrong.

"Callie? Is everything all right? Did you have a problem with the printer? It can be temperamental—"

He didn't even get to finish the sentence before she burst into tears. The next thing he knew, she was in his arms, sobbing into his shoulder—and he wasn't sure whether she'd moved into him, or if he'd moved into her.

But it didn't matter in the least.

He was holding Callie—a damp, soggy Callie, but Callie nonetheless.

"Shhh...it's all right," he said, allowing himself to stroke the length of her back, forcing himself to stop just above her ass—and not at all sure what he was soothing her about...and whether it *would* be okay. "Shhhh...shhh..."

She was warm and soft and curvy and smelled so sweet and delicious that he didn't care that she was getting tears and snot all over his sweater—which didn't happen to be one of his favorites, but it had been recently dry-cleaned.

"I've decided I'm...going to have to...call off the... wedding." She gulped when she pulled away a little bit, sobbed a little more. "I...it's the only...right...thing to do..."

You are not going to be excited about this, he told himself firmly, even as his heart gave a little leap. *Just because she's canceling the wedding because she doesn't want to* die *during it doesn't mean anything.*

It just means she doesn't want to die.

"Oh, Callie, I'm so sorry," he said. "I really am." He really was. Because she was bereft and heartbroken and obviously the decision was a difficult one.

She didn't sob for very long, he'd give her credit for that— just long enough that he could feel the dampness through the sweater *and* the button-down shirt he wore beneath it—but even once she settled down a little, she didn't seem interested in putting any proper space between them.

The next thing he knew, he found himself sitting next to her on the couch, Callie tucked up against him, his arm around her waist, as she sighed and sniffled and wiped her nose.

"Sometimes it sucks being an adult," she said. "You know?"

"Yeah. I know." He resisted the urge to stroke her along the arm, and he was *very* aware of the fact that her soft, generous breast was resting against his chest. It felt like it was burning into his side, and he knew exactly where her hip was too, because it was bumping against his hip.

She just needs a friend right now, he told himself. *Like in When Harry Met—oh, no, no, no... that is* not *a good comparison at all.*

"Want to watch something?" she asked in a low, scratchy voice—surely unconsciously echoing a line from that very movie after the scene that this very moment sort of reminded him of.

Dammit.

"I just need some distraction. Or—oh, no—do you have work to do?" she added quickly, pulling away a little to look at him. "You must have lots to do with it being year end. I should get going. I didn't realize how late it is!"

"No, no, that would be good," he replied before she could straighten up all the way. He'd sit here all night unmoving if it meant he could cuddle Callie Quigley. Work could wait, and keeping a guy's circulation moving was overrated. "I mean, watching something is a good idea—I'd hate to waste that fire. And besides, the weather outside is frightful."

He felt her chuckle a little next to him, even felt her cheek move against his arm—that was how sensitized he was to her every breath. "Is it cold outside, baby?" she asked with a little giggle.

"It's definitely cold outside, but it's nice and warm in

here," he said, unable to suppress his own low rumble of a chuckle.

"The fire is slowly dying," she whispered over another adorable giggle.

"It is *not*," he said with mock indignation. "I just stoked up that baby, and when I get a fire going, she burns for *hours*."

For some reason, those words hung in the air, settling in the silence, and Ben felt acutely aware of the double meaning one could read in them. If one should be thinking down that path.

Which...damn. He needed to shift a little—things were getting a bit tight in his chinos—but he dared not move. Not now.

Somehow, Callie managed to grab the TV remote and manipulate it, and the next thing he knew she'd landed on *When Harry Met Sally...*

"Ooh! I love this one. It's one of my favorite holiday movies—even though most people don't think of it as a holiday movie. But so many of the pivotal scenes happen during the holidays," she said. "Mind if we watch it? It's a comfort-watch for me, you know."

"Sure," he managed to say, wondering not only how he was going to get through a whole movie about friends falling in love, but also that famous "I'll have what she's having" scene with Callie bundled up next to him all the while.

But somehow he managed it, and even enjoyed it. Why not, since this sort of perfect, fantasy idyll would never happen again?

And when, during the scene with "I Could Write a Book" on

the soundtrack, he heard the soft, delicate snore coming from the woman next to him, he smiled indulgently...and he was finally, *finally*, able to touch the soft, bright lock of hair that fell over his arm. It crackled with static electricity and gave him a little shock as Harry Connick, Jr., sang about making two lovers of friends.

But Ben didn't care.

And pretty soon, he lapsed into sleep as well.

When Callie opened her eyes, it took her a moment to figure out where she was.

And then, slowly it dawned on her that the large, solid warmth next to her was *Ben Tremaine*.

And they were on his couch.

And she'd been really cuddled up with him. Practically in his lap.

Her face flamed when she realized *where her hand was*.

Oh my God, she thought, and began to gingerly pull her fingers away from where they'd nestled...in his *lap*. Like, down around a thigh...

How did that happen?

Ben's eyes opened just as she fully extricated herself from him, and for a moment she was trapped by his gaze.

He looked like he was about to say something, but she didn't give him the chance—oh, boy, was she embarrassed. She'd practically *thrown* herself at him last night—and if picking *When Harry Met Sally...* to watch wasn't enough of a hint for that big lug, then she wasn't even going to give him another thought.

Or...even worse...maybe he *had* got the hint, and just didn't want to take it.

Because she figured she had been pretty obvious.

And since he didn't walk through that wide-open door, it was clear he was *not* interested in her in that way.

Period. End of story.

"Oh, wow," she said, feeling very awkward. "I didn't mean to fall asleep like that." God, she needed a toothbrush. Even in her wildest fantasies, she hadn't imagined staying the night at Ben's last night.

"Me neither," he said, shifting around then pulling to his feet. "But that's okay. It's nearly five-thirty. Uh...I can make some coffee. Do you want to—uh—freshen up? There's an extra toothbrush in the right hand drawer in the bathroom."

Of course there was.

He was, after all, Ben Tremaine.

CHAPTER 7

"THERE'S REALLY ONLY ONE SOLUTION," said Iva Bergstrom, looking around the table at her friends, with her attention finally landing on Callie.

Iva was in her late sixties, and she was petite and neat and so darling that Callie had privately described her as a delicious apple puff of a woman. Her cheeks were always flushed perfectly pink—quite likely due to a skillful application of blusher—and her hair was a pure white cotton poof. She dressed the same way she probably had during her career as a librarian: in twinset cardigans and nice slacks, usually in bright colors that matched her jewelry.

The Tuesday Ladies, as they were known—and not necessarily because that was the day they gathered on; they met up nearly every day, and usually here at Orbra's Tea House—were ensconced at their regular table in the front window of the place. It was large and round, with plenty of room for all five of them plus one or two others who might join their clique—in this case, Callie and another Wicks Hollow local, Fiona Murphy.

It was after eight p.m. on the 21st of December, and since the tea house closed at five every day, all the other customers were gone. As usual, a team of bakers worked in the back, preparing fresh quiches, tarts, scones, gingerbread houses, and more for tomorrow's menu, but the rest of the place was empty and quiet.

"You tell'er, sister." Maxine Took, the self-appointed leader of the Tuesday Ladies, thumped her ever-present cane and nodded vehemently. Her shiny, impossibly thick dark hair didn't move at all, either because it was a wig or because she used an entire can of hairspray every time she did her hair. No one was certain which, and no one was about to ask the acerbic octogenarian.

"Let the poor woman *talk*," said Juanita Acerita, Maxine's best frenemy. After her husband died, she'd sold the small chain of high-end Mexican restaurants she'd started thirty years ago, and now played Scrabble with Maxine when she wasn't trying to maneuver the town veterinarian into becoming the second Mr. Acerita.

Tonight she held a large tote on her lap, and from inside two large, furry, butterfly-shaped ears poked up. Between them was a pair of sharp, beady black eyes and, below, the cutest canine button nose Callie had ever seen. The little dog, whose name was Bruce Banner, was eyeing the piece of gingerbread house that Juanita was munching. "Honestly, Maxine, if you'd just keep your mouth closed for more than a minute—"

"Well, we all know what the solution is," Maxine groused. "Why does she have to create so much drama when she's introducing it? Orbry, are you bringing some more of those cinnamon scones?" she called as Orbra came into sight with a laden tea cart. "Juanita's been feeding them to her dog—"

"I have not," said her friend, looking around guiltily, because, of course, she had been. Callie had seen her do it when she thought no one was watching. She smothered a smile.

"I mean, it is quite obvious," said the fourth Tuesday Lady, a slender, youthful sixty-something woman. She had short, platinum blond hair and a compact, muscular body. Cherry Wilder was the owner of the yoga studio in Wicks Hollow and had arrived just after one of her classes and so was dressed the part. "What to do about Iva's wedding."

"Of course. There's really only one solution to the problem," Juanita said agreeably.

Callie sat next to Iva, nervously waiting for what the actual solution *was*.

Callie had called her client on the way back from Ben's house to Grand Rapids last week, and told Hollis Nath that she was going to cancel the wedding—at least as currently planned. To make up for it, she promised she would do all of the planning and cover all of the services herself (yikes! that would mean the cost of *two* weddings for the Bergstrom/Nath couple when all was said and done because there were no refunds at this late date) for the reschedule.

But it was the only thing she could think of to do. No amount of publicity or marketing was worth anyone's safety—and, as she'd been reminded more than once, it *was* Wicks Hollow.

You couldn't ignore the supernatural or the otherworldly here. And that was where Callie had made her first mistake: thinking she could.

But although Mr. Nath had been very gracious and understanding about the situation, Callie hadn't spoken to Iva herself about it...until now, when Iva had requested her to meet up at the tea house tonight. Even though she'd been super busy, Callie had juggled her schedule to be here, and she'd conscripted Fiona into coming with her because she knew Fiona and Iva were very close...and honestly, because she was a little nervous about what Iva was going to say.

I mean, what do *you say to the wedding planner who cancels on you ten days before your wedding?* she'd said to Fiona. *I'll be lucky if I ever work in event planning again.*

"How about some warm-ups?" said Orbra van Hest cheerily as she wheeled up a tea cart. The owner of the tea house and the fifth Tuesday Lady, she was in her early seventies. Robust, solid, and very Dutch with iron gray hair and a will to match, she loomed over six feet tall and ran her establishment with skill and finesse. Even Trib eagerly took advice from Orbra. "Now, Iva, you're going to have to back up and fill me in on some of this—I've been busy closing down in the back."

"Callie's canceled the wedding on her," Maxine informed her. "Just called her out of the blue and yanked the rug out from under the poor dear!"

Callie's face went hot, and she squirmed in her chair, trying to figure out how to defend herself—but there *was* no defense. She had *really* screwed up. Before she could speak, Fiona patted her hand and murmured, "Shh. Don't worry. That's just Maxine."

"What're you two whispering about over there?" snapped Maxine, leaning across the table so sharply the cups rattled in their saucers. "I can hear everything you're saying, you know."

"Then I'm sure you heard me say how everyone listens to what you say," Fiona replied sweetly. "And no one would dream of arguing with you."

"That's right," Maxine retorted. She gave a vehement nod as if it were the exclamation point of her sentence and the cups rattled again.

Callie couldn't help fidgeting. Why was she here, and what was Iva's big solution?

"Oooh! Orbra!" Cherry had lifted the quilted tea cozy off one of the teapots only to discover it wasn't a teapot at all, but a bottle of Crown Royal. "When you said warm-ups, I didn't realize you were serious!"

"I really like a good dollop in the cinnamon blend tea," Orbra said with a crafty smile. "But it would also be good in the pu'erh. if you don't mind the caffeine. And add a nice helping of honey, too, while you're at it. Now, there's some Bailey's under there somewhere—you can put it in the chai or the vanilla oolong. *And* I've got my Honeybear syrup—you know how good that is in a hot toddy!"

"Honeybear syrup?" asked Fiona. "You know I'm a vegetarian, Orbra..."

"There's no *bear* in it," Maxine said with an eyeroll. "It's got—what is it, Orbry?"

"It's a syrup you can add to whiskey or tea—or both, if you like—which I do—and it's got orange, sage, and honey in it."

"Anyway," said Iva, picking up the story as Orbra finally sat down, "As I was—I mean, as *Maxine* was saying, Callie decided it might be best not to move forward with having our wedding outside on the Tremaine Tower balcony because of the curse. She doesn't want to risk anyone's life, do you?" She reached over and patted Callie's hand, her blue eyes bright and sympathetic.

"It's just as well," said Orbra. "Who wants an *outdoor* wedding in Michigan in December anyway?"

"But *I* do," said Iva earnestly. "I always wanted to get married on New Year's Eve—and how many people do you know get married *outside* on New Year's Eve?"

"Only the crazy ones," muttered Maxine, eyeing the pile of cinnamon scones.

"Then call me crazy, but Callie really sold me on the idea of an outside wedding in December. It's so unique, and it would be beautiful—"

"But the curse—" Juanita started.

"So don't have it at Tremaine Tower," said Cherry, pouring a healthy glut of Crown Royal into her mug. "And pray for decent weather."

"You always have to pray for decent weather when you're getting married outside," said Juanita. "Practically speaking. And—"

"Only the *crazy ones*," said Maxine again, a bit louder.

"Oh, hush up and drink this," said Cherry, shoving the Crown-Royal-laden teacup at her friend. "Let Iva finish."

"You've been interrupting her just as much—"

"Please. Ladies, Callie's not used to you all, and she's about to have a heart attack," said Fiona with a giggle.

"Well give her some of this," said Maxine, gesturing to her brandied drink. "Needs more honey, Cherry."

"And a cherry would be good too," said Juanita, perking up. "Cherry, can you put in a cherry too?" She tittered and

Callie wondered if Juanita had already tasted some of the Crown Royal. Or something else.

But Fiona was right—she was sitting here with her belly going in knots waiting to hear what her client, Iva, was going to say about the wedding situation.

"All right, everyone listen up!" Iva had pulled to her feet and she looked around the table. "No talking for five minutes —that includes you, Maxine. *And* you, Juanita."

"Blah, blah," muttered Maxine. But she closed her mouth after that.

"It's very simple. I've decided I want to have my wedding outside on the balcony at the clock tower as planned," Iva went on primly. "It's going to be absolutely stunning the way Callie has designed and described it—and we have plans for every weather eventuality *except* if there's a crazy blizzard. The nice thing about precipitation for winter weddings is that, unlike with rain, snow is pretty and it doesn't necessarily ruin things because it's not wet—it just freezes. *Maxine, I said five minutes.* And so," she went on as if she hadn't digressed, "I've decided there's only one way to proceed in order for me and Hollis to have the gorgeous nuptials we've talked about. So, we have to fix things up with Brenda Tremaine."

Iva looked right at Callie. "We're going to have a séance."

CHAPTER 8

"I CAN'T BELIEVE they talked me into this," Callie hissed into Fiona's ear as they began to climb up the steps inside the clock tower. "This is *insane*."

"I can't believe you insisted I come too," her friend replied. But her eyes danced and she looked remarkably at ease considering the fact that Maxine Took, of all people, was going to be the medium for the séance. "Besides, I did a palm reading on Iva the other day. She definitely has a marriage line, and her life line is long enough. I don't think she's going to die at her wedding."

"Well that's comforting," Callie muttered.

"Hurry up you two," ordered Maxine, who somehow had managed to push her way ahead of everyone and was at the top of the stairs, walking stick in hand.

That was when it dawned on Callie that the walking stick was more of a prop than an ambulatory aid.

"Now, Brucie, you're going to have to be quiet during this whole thing," Juanita was saying as she made her way up a bit more slowly than her counterpart.

"She's bringing her *dog*?" Callie whispered to Fiona. "Isn't that going to...ruin things?"

"Well, you know animals are more sensitive to these sorts of things," Fiona replied. "My cat Gretchen definitely was."

"I've got the Ouija board," said Iva, puffing a little as she caught up to Callie and Fiona on the steps. "I'm not sure if we're going to need it, but just in case."

"We don't need no Wee-jah board," Maxine called down. "I've got my own way, talking to the spirits."

"That's 'cause you're a witchy woman," snickered Juanita, and she and Cherry began to sing the refrain from the old Eagles song.

"Besides," Maxine continued as the oooh-ooohs echoed in the stairwell, "I asked Jean to be here, so she can interpret for us."

"Who's Jean?" asked Callie, really wishing she'd just stayed in Grand Rapids tonight.

She knew what to expect. These poor little old ladies wouldn't stand a chance against the angry, violent Brenda Tremaine and the fake cranberry champagne cocktail stuff she was always flinging around. That was why Callie had let herself be talked into coming—someone had to be there to save them.

"Oh, Jean is their friend who died—actually, she was murdered—two summers ago. She was the sixth Tuesday Lady, and after her death, she came back and haunted her niece[1] until she figured out Jean had been murdered and helped to catch her killer. It was before I moved here, but I heard all about it," said Fiona.

"That's right," said Orbra, who'd brought up the rear of the climbers. "Like I said before, if anyone was ever going to haunt anyone, it would be Jean Fickler. That was a good idea to invite her tonight, Maxine," she called up. "It'll be just like old times with the six of us together again."

Finally, they all got to the top and Callie opened the door to the room. It was just as clean and quiet and still as it had been last week, before she pissed off Brenda Tremaine and got caught in the tornado of her fury. And the chairs and cocktail tables she'd ordered for the reception and forgotten to cancel had been delivered. Just lovely. Another fee she was going to have to eat.

The heat wasn't on, so the air was chill. They were going to have to remain in their coats and hats. Callie wished—briefly—for a fire like the one she'd enjoyed at Ben's last week.

Then she quickly shut down that thought.

"All right, Brucie, you're going to have to sit on Mommy's lap and be very good," said Juanita, gently extricating the small dog from his tote.

"Everyone sit in a circle," ordered Maxine. "We need chairs. Get some chairs."

"Get your own chair," Juanita grumbled.

She tucked Bruce Banner under one arm and began to muscle a cushioned, upholstered chair to the center of the room. Callie shook her head as the other ladies scraped and dragged chairs from the stacks against the wall. There were multitudes of cold breaths puffing around, grunts and groans and loud scraping sounds.

"We need a table," Maxine said after all of the chairs had been arranged—which then meant the chairs had to be moved in order to fit the table through.

Callie rolled her eyes as she and Fiona carried the table over. This was going to be a cluster-freak of the highest order.

"I've got the candles," said Cherry, and she and Iva began to arrange ten candles in the center of the table. "And some incense that will help to soothe our minds and open our sixth chakras as we welcome Brenda Tremaine's spirit to our circle tonight."

"This is surreal," Callie murmured as she took a chair next to Fiona.

"It's going to be fascinating," replied her friend as she arranged her flowing skirts and long parka over her legs.

"All right, everyone *shush*," Maxine said as the candles were lit. "Now, we're going to all be silent—especially you, Neety—and your little dog too!" She cackled a little and Callie couldn't control her own giggle as Cherry muttered, "Spoken like a true witch."

"She's not really a witch is she?" Callie asked Fiona, suddenly nervous. It was, after all, Wicks Hollow.

"No one's ever said she was," Fiona replied off-handedly. "But no one's ever said she isn't. But besides, witches aren't necessarily mediums. They don't do séances."

"I wouldn't put it past her—"

"*Hush*," Maxine said, and there was something different about her voice. It was strong and calm without being as sharp and annoying as it usually was. "Shhhh. Everyone quiet down and let's hold hands, all right? Bare hands—take off your gloves."

Callie couldn't help but glance at the picture of Brenda Tremaine, which was directly across the room from where she was sitting. Fiona took one of her hands, and Cherry took the other. Maxine sat across from her, with Iva on one side and Juanita on the other. Orbra sat between Cherry and Iva.

The room fell silent and Callie felt an icy shiver run down her spine. Could have been from the fact that it was after dark on a December day and they were in a room with no heat...or it could have been because she was more than a little nervous.

The candle flames swayed and bounced casually and Callie found herself staring at the dancing lights. The scent of the incense Cherry had lit smelled nice, and Callie relaxed a little as she breathed slowly in and out.

"Now...we welcome any benign and benevolent spirits that wish to join us tonight," said Maxine. "On this Winter Solstice..."

Callie's eyes popped open and she looked at Fiona, but her friend's eyes were softly closed and her face seemed peaceful in its repose.

Winter Solstice...that was a Wiccan celebration, wasn't it? Maybe Maxine really *was* a witch.

"If you are here, please make your presence known." Maxine's voice continued to be smooth and almost hypnotic. "Jean, that includes you," she added a little more abruptly. Cherry suppressed a soft snort but immediately subsided.

Callie felt the air move and her eyes opened again. Try as she might, she was not going to be able to keep them closed. She looked up at Brenda Tremaine's portrait and gave a quiet gasp when she thought she saw the woman's hair moving as if in a breeze. She blinked, and then the impression was gone.

Maxine spoke again, "Jean Fickler, if you're there, please—"

Thunk!

Callie's attention whipped to the window, but nothing was there.

Thunkity-thunk!

"So you remember our special knock, do you, Jean?" Maxine said. There was a smile in her voice, though it was a little too dark for Callie to see it on her face.

Thunk-thunkity-thunk!

"Yes, it's definitely you. I hope you're doing well over there on the other side."

Thu-unk!

"Glad to hear it! Well, I'm sure it'll be a long time before I'm ready to join you, but it's nice to hear all is well up there. Now, we need your otherworldly help with a problem. Iva wants to get married—"

Thunk! Thunk! THUNK!!

"I know, I know," Maxine went on. "She swore she never would, but then Mr. Right came along and she threw all her feminism out the window—"

"That's *not* true," Iva hissed. "Don't be telling Jean that!"

"Well, you can't deny Hollis came along and swept you off your feet," Juanita said practically. "And—"

"I swept *him* off *his* feet," Iva retorted, a little louder now. "And we've been together almost two years now, and we just decided for practical reasons that it makes sense to join our households. Don't be shaking your ghostly finger at me, Jean Fickler," she added, looking up and around the room. "You were happily married for a couple of decades."

Thunkkkkk...

"*Anyway,*" Maxine said, her voice taking on its regular, strident tone. "Iva wants to get married here on New Year's

Eve, Jean, and one of your co-ghosts seems to have a bug up her supernatural butt about—"

Brenda's portrait crashed to the floor, and everyone jumped except Callie, who'd seen it fall. But Maxine was the only person who didn't turn to look, even though her back was to the painting.

"Well, it seems Brenda has decided to join us," Maxine said matter-of-factly. "Welcome, Bren—"

The other portrait fell off the wall, and then the wind inside the room suddenly whipped up in what was becoming a familiar scene to Callie. She held on to Fiona's and Cherry's hands as the spectral storm rose. The gale churned and thrashed them as they sat in their protective circle, gripping each other's hands tightly.

The room was suddenly frigidly cold, and their breaths came out in white bursts as the candles jolted and leapt and finally guttered into nothing. Darkness closed in on them, coming from within the room and from the wintry outside on this, the longest night of the year.

Callie felt the wet spray on her face and the small, angry pelting of phantasmic cranberry cocktail, and she heard the quiet whine from Bruce Banner.

"Hold on," Maxine said, her voice deep and calm and powerful as Brenda's wrath battered them. "Hold on!"

They held on for what seemed like forever.

And then at last the volley of wind and hail slowed, then eased away. Callie could hear her companions panting a little as quiet descended. Bruce Banner whined again, just once, then subsided into silence.

"That was quite an entrance, Brenda," Maxine said. "Even I don't make entrances like that! Now, don't get all riled up again, Brenda. We aren't here to bother you—we just want to help put you to rest."

If Callie hadn't known it was Maxine Took doing the talking, she would never have believed it...the voice was more smooth and reasonable than before. Maybe Maxine was possessed by this Jean Fickler's spirit.

"Iva here wants to get married on your balcony on New Year's Eve," Maxine went on. Her eyes were wide in her dark face. "She is asking your permission to do so, and we request your cooperation for the evening. Will you give it?"

It felt like an earthquake.

The room shook and the entire tower seemed to sway. The stacks of chairs against the wall rattled, and Bruce Banner began to whine piteously.

"What is wrong?" demanded Maxine. "Why are you so angry, Brenda?"

The walls shook more violently and Callie was actually afraid Tremaine Tower might come down. She squeezed Fiona's hand tightly and looked at the others around the circle. None of them had their eyes closed—in fact, the whites of everyone's eyes were somehow reflected in the darkness.

"Brenda Tremaine, I call upon you to cease your bitching and complaining and leave this place!" cried Maxine. "Or at least, cease your bitching and complaining so we can have a wedding here!"

Brenda didn't respond immediately, but Callie felt the shaking and vibrating ease a little. And then a little more. And then more.

And finally, it was quiet again. The only sound was the very low whining from Bruce, and a very normal wintery wind buffeting the *outside* of the building.

"Well, that was interesting," said Orbra, speaking for the first time.

Thunk-thunkity-thunk!

"Jean?" said Juanita.

Thunk-thunk!

"Jean must have done something to calm her down," Cherry muttered.

"Took her long enough," crabbed Maxine, back to true form. "Someone light the damned candles again, will you? Can't see a blasted thing."

"I wonder if she's really gone," said Iva as Cherry lit the candles. One by one, the flames began to sway and bounce normally on their wicks. That alone told Callie that things were back to normal.

"There's no real way to know..." Fiona's voice trailed off. "Oh. Maybe there is."

She pointed wordlessly to the wall where Brenda's portrait used to hang.

Scrawled on it in rickety, barely legible red lettering was:

FAR WELL

WARE RAIL

---

1. *Sinister Summer*

CHAPTER 9

"WHAT THE HELL DOES THAT MEAN?" Cherry said.

"Looks like gibberish to me," Maxine grumbled, thumping over with her cane to look more closely at Brenda Tremaine's message. Callie followed her and shined her mobile phone light on the wall.

"Far-well-ware-rail? What is that? Some sort of word puzzle?" Orbra sounded annoyed.

"You know, Jean, if you were going to help us, you coulda made sure she wrote something that actually *meant* something," Maxine said, planting her free hand on her hip.

Thunk!! Thunk!!

"Whatever," Maxine sneered. "See if I call your ghostly butt into my next séance."

THUNK!!!

"I guess it's a good thing Jean hasn't learned the whole indoor-tornado technique yet," Fiona muttered to Callie, who couldn't keep from laughing. The whole situation was just ludicrous...and as far as she was concerned, nothing was really resolved. "And what's that red stuff that's splashed all over your face—and mine too, I assume? That's from Brenda?"

Callie nodded. "It washes off. I think it's a throw back to the cranberry champagne cocktail she was holding when she died, and guessing she used whatever it is to write her message."

"Well, now, let's just calm down and take a minute to see if we can decipher Brenda's message," said Iva in her prim, librarian voice. She probably had no idea her face was covered in blood-red streaks as well. "And not go around insulting specters and phantoms, shall we, Maxine?"

"It's not like they didn't speak English when they were living," Maxine grumbled. "Where'd she go to school anyway?" But Callie noticed her sharp eyes were fixed on the words and she could almost hear the wheels moving in the curmudgeonly woman's brain.

"All right, so let's just take it one little bit at a time," said Cherry. "Far...well...ware...rail. It's a little bit of a tongue twister..."

"Far well could be 'farewell'," said Juanita, who was cuddling a much happier Bruce to her ample chest. "She just missed a letter. Maybe she's saying goodbye."

"Good point," said Orbra. "You did ask her to leave, Maxine," she reminded her friend.

"She didn't ask, she *ordered*," Juanita said.

"True dat," Maxine admitted.

"So she's saying farewell, is she? That bodes well for your wedding coming off, doesn't it, Iva?" said Cherry.

"I like it. Jean, we need an interpreter. Is she saying farewell?" asked Iva.

Thunk.

"Since it wasn't a vehement you're-on-the-wrong-track thunk, I'll take that as a yes. So that's good. The wedding is *on!*" Iva beamed at everyone, spreading her arms wide. "I can't wait to tell Hollis! He's going to be so excited—and nervous. I've never seen a man so nervous about getting married in my life—and it's going to be his *fourth* wedding! You'd think he'd be used to it by now." Her cheeks were pink behind the red streaks and her eyes positively sparkled.

Callie *really* hoped Iva was right.

"But what about the rest of it? Don't forget, Brenda was around in the 1920s, so we need to think about common vernacular back then." Cherry said, standing in front of the wall again. "Ware...rail. Ware...rail. Waril? Whirl? Hmmm. War?"

"Ware could be from beware," said Juanita. "Isn't that an old-fashioned way of giving a warning? Ware those who step on a gravestone, yada yada?"

"Could be," mused Iva, who clearly didn't like the idea of a warning. "What about rail?"

"Rail. Well, there's a railway station out there—or used to be—and the tracks go by right below. And there's a rail going up the stairs—*and* a rail on the balcony," said Orbra. "She did die on the balcony, don't forget."

"Maybe she missed another letter and it was supposed to be trail," mused Cherry.

"Or rain, instead of rail—oh, that could make sense. She's warning about rain on the balcony during your wedding, Iva," said Orbra.

"Oooh. That could be—"

"But it's winter. It's probably not going to rain in December. Why wouldn't she say snow or ice instead of rain?" said Fiona.

"Maybe she was trying to cover all bases," said Juanita.

"There's also rail, as in a night rail—an old-fashioned word for nightgown," said Iva in her sweet, prim voice. "Maybe she mixed up the words—homophones give lots of people trouble—and meant to say 'wear' as in w-e-a-r—wear a rail. Which is what I definitely *don't* plan to do on my wedding night," she added with a mischievous grin and a deeper blush.

The ladies burst out laughing, and even though Callie felt like it might be a little TMI, she couldn't help joining in. Iva really was the most likable, lovely woman.

And Callie really didn't want her wedding to be a disaster—or, worse, a tragedy.

"All right, then...she's leaving, so the wedding is on. Iva should not wear a nightrail on her wedding night, and should beware of rain, and maybe beware of a train or the rail. I think that about covers it," said Cherry.

"The most important thing is: the wedding is *on!*" Iva said, then she whirled to Callie. "You got that? So you'd better get cracking, young lady!"

"I do love my family, but I've had my fill of them for a while," said Jake DeRiccio. "A solid week of holiday stuff and I'm done. Between Pops and my sisters...yep, that's it. Over and *out*. Thank God it's the 27th and all the parties and family obligations are over."

Ben grinned and nodded. "I feel you, man. And I only have one sister to deal with—plus my mom."

He loved his family—he really did—but he was also used to living alone and having a relatively quiet, stable life. He was in complete agreement with Jake that more than two days of family-holiday stuff—especially when there were a half-dozen nieces and nephews who were hopped up on candy and cookies and presents and who loved to play "Pile On Uncle Ben" after he'd eaten a very large meal. Or two. One of the girls had even decided his beard needed decorating.

Ben was still shedding glitter two days later.

"Declan's still in the honeymoon phase with his new woman," teased Jake. "We had to practically drag him out for Trivia Night—he wanted to stay home and play Trivial Pursuit with his hottie Leslie instead of coming out and helping us retain our championship title here."

"Well, since the way Leslie and I play trivia is a lot different from Trivia Night here with you bozos, who can blame me?" retorted Declan, looking around the Roost. "But it worked out because Les flew back to Philadelphia to see her mom for a few days. She'll be back in time for New Year's Eve."

"What do you mean, how *you* play Trivia Night?" asked Ben as he sipped a B-Cubed beer.

Declan gave them a sly look as the Trivia Night emcee came by to collect their team's signup sheet. "We like to play Strip Trivial Pursuit. Every time one of us gets a wedge piece, the other one has to take off an article of clothing."

"Well, that would only work if you started with no more than six articles of clothing," Ben pointed out.

"Precisely. No extra layers allowed." Declan grinned. "Socks count as two."

"That is brilliant," Ben replied, grinning. Then his grin faded a little. Not for the first time, he wished he had someone to play Trivial Pursuit with—and not, as Declan said earlier, with these clowns.

That whole missing-out-on-life feeling had really settled in for him over the last week of family holiday stuff. He'd felt his singleness more acutely than he'd ever done before...and the fact that he'd blown his shot with Callie made it worse. Maybe he wouldn't have been so bummed about it if he hadn't had that evening with her—that time that reminded him just how much he really liked being around her. How much he wished he'd had the balls to pursue her back in high school and every time he'd seen her since then.

"All right everyone, tonight's first category is *Star Wars,*" said the emcee. "There'll be ten questions in the category, from easy to most difficult."

Declan, Jake, and Baxter—who'd just slipped into his chair—hooted and cheered. They knew with Ben on their team, there was nothing about *Star Wars* he didn't know or have an opinion on.

"That's not fair," grumbled Maxine Took loudly. She was sitting with her cohorts the Tuesday Ladies at the next table. Along with them was Jake's widowed father, Ricky. "Cherry's not here tonight, and we the rest of us don't know nothing about that Yodi stuff. You-all better send Benny or Baxter over here to help us old farts."

"Go on, Ben," said Baxter quickly. "You heard Maxine."

"Don't send Ben," exclaimed Jake. "I don't know anything about *Star Wars.*"

"Seriously? How can you not know anything about *Star Wars* unless you're eighty years old and think Yoda is a class Cherry Wilder teaches?" replied Baxter.

"I heard that, Baxter James," snapped Maxine. "Now one of you cheeky boys needs to come on over here and help us old ladies. It's be kind to your elders week."

"Who told them about Trivia Night?" Declan whispered desperately. "I thought the whole town promised to keep it a secret."

"Ben did," said Juanita, who had somehow managed to smuggle in her tote bag with the little dog. She beamed at them from behind a pile of nachos with what looked like extra cheese. "He was into the tea shop, meeting with Orbra about her year-end stuff and told us."

"You told them?" Baxter goggled at Ben. "Why would you do that? Why? Why would you ruin the peacefulness and serenity of Trivia Night that way?"

"You and Ricky could switch teams," suggested Iva Bergstrom, who Ben thought was the cutest, most darling grandmother-like lady of the group.

Everyone in the Roost was looking at them, and it was clear to Ben that the game wasn't going to start until Maxine was satisfied.

"You guys owe me," he said to his traitorous friends. "Better keep my glass full over there, you hear?" When he rose, the entire bar erupted in applause and cheers. "And the rest of you better get me your year-end projections," he announced to the room at large. "*Tomorrow.*"

Half the people in the room groaned, and he laughed as he sank into the chair that had been vacated by Jake's dad.

"All right ladies," he said, grinning at his new team. "We're going to kick some butt."

And they did. With Trivia King Ben's help, the Tuesday Ladies team handily won the first round on *Star Wars*, capping off a ten for ten score because Ben knew that Chewbacca had died when a moon fell on him in the Extended Universe novels.

The second round's topic, which was the 1970s, was obviously a piece of cake for Maxine, Orbra, Iva, and Juanita.

By that time, Ben's former teammates were begging him to come back to their table.

"If you help them win, we'll *never* get rid of them," hissed Baxter from his seat. "They'll be here every Tuesday."

"Oh well," Ben replied with a shrug. He'd been enjoying the company of the ladies—and the beer he kept reordering on Baxter's and Declan's tabs. "I like to be on the winning team."

"Now, Ben," said Iva Bergstrom, patting his hand during the break between rounds two and three, "I just want to tell you how nice it was for your family to let the wedding go on over at the clock tower. Considering all the history."

He lowered his beer and looked at her. "The wedding? At the clock tower?"

Since that strange and awkward morning over a week ago when he'd awakened with Callie tucked up against him and her hand cupping his crotch, he'd tried hard not to think too much about her.

He'd dismissed the sliver of hope that maybe by her canceling the wedding somehow it might end up being a permanent cancellation. Which wasn't very nice of him and he knew it, which was why he didn't let himself give it more than a passing thought...at least, not more than once a day.

Instead, he congratulated himself on being the perfect gentleman during their unexpected sleepover. And he'd tried to think about how sad and disappointed Callie must be feeling about having to cancel her wedding.

He had one sister, but that was enough for him to be very clear on how important weddings were for most women. And based on the way she'd waxed rhapsodic about glittery white tree forests and hurricanes and ecru lace (whatever ecru was), he suspected Callie was definitely one of those women who put a lot of importance on her wedding.

"Yes, dear. Oh, maybe you've been too busy doing everyone's taxes to pay attention to it," said Iva with a little laugh. Her blue eyes sparkled and her cheeks flushed little pink.

"I thought—I thought Callie had canceled the wedding," Ben said, very relieved when another beer appeared at his elbow. Apparently Kendra had taken him at his word when he said to keep them coming. "She told me she was going to cancel it."

"Oh, she tried to. But I wouldn't let her," Iva said.

"No, we weren't having any of your great-great-aunt's Bridezilla tactics," put in Maxine. "That Brenda is a real Bridezilla—you know, she's like a monster when it comes to her wedding," she said, obviously recently having learned the term. "We went over there and I set that Ghostzilla—hey, I like that word—straight."

"Who?" Ben asked, feeling like his brain had suddenly begun to ooze from his ears.

"Brenda Tremaine's ghost, of course," said Juanita. "We had a séance."

"You had what?" Ben said faintly. It was far too loud and raucous in the Roost, because he surely he hadn't heard her correctly.

"A séance," replied Iva. "We had a séance and spoke to Brenda—as well as our old friend Jean Fickler, who died two summers ago with the help of a murderous culprit—and Brenda told us farewell. So obviously she's not going to interfere or curse me at my wedding. So it's on." She was beaming as if she'd just announced her first grandchild.

Ben was still trying to wade through the trough of astonishing information Iva Bergstrom had just dumped on him when his mind zeroed in on one phrase.

And then the world stopped. The noise and chaos in the dive bar ebbed away. He felt suddenly very, very still. "*Your* wedding?"

"Why, yes," Iva replied. Her eyes latched solemnly onto his.

"It's *your* wedding? On New Year's Eve at the tower? *This* New Year's Eve?"

"Yes, Ben. My wedding. To Hollis. You've met him before, haven't you? He's been after me for over two years to put a ring on it, and I finally..."

But Ben hadn't heard anything after the first four words. Iva Bergstrom's wedding.

Not Callie's wedding?

He didn't understand.

He just didn't understand.

But what he did know was that a sudden blooming, blossoming, billowing warmth of hope was spreading through him.

"Whose wedding did you think it was?" Iva asked, still fixing him with her steady, birdlike gaze.

"I...uh...thought it was Callie Quigley who was getting married," he managed to say...just as he remembered—he *remembered, now,* after weeks of stupidity and unnecessary chivalry—how Trib had been telling him how Callie had started her own business in events planning after managing all the events at the ritzy Amway Grand Hotel in Grand Rapids...

Stupid. Stupid. Stupid.

"Ben, are you all right?" Iva's soft wrinkled hand was pressing onto the back of his wrist.

And then he smiled. And felt suddenly quite lighter.

"Yes, I am," he replied. "I most definitely am."

CHAPTER 10

NEW YEAR'S Eve was a whirlwind for Callie.

She'd arrived in Wicks Hollow the night before and stayed at her Uncle Trib's house so she could start the day early and give her full attention to the Bergstrom/Nath wedding.

The weather, at least, was cooperating. It was supposed to be crisp, clear, and just around thirty-five degrees into the evening. There was a fresh snowfall from the night before that blanketed everything with a virginal white. She couldn't have planned it better if she'd been Mother Nature herself.

Callie was at Tremaine Tower by eight a.m., supervising the installation of the forest of bare white branches on the balcony. Twenty huge, gorgeous, glittery branches were placed upright in Christmas tree holders along the front of the balcony, and filling in behind in staggered rows.

Tiny lights were strung on random trees, but not all of them (Callie didn't subscribe to what she called the "matchy-matchy" design mindset—where everything had to be identical or to match perfectly), in order to give the appearance of a fairytale forest. She hung swags made from arborvitae, spruce, and holly bush along the front of the balcony railing, then wove ecru and champagne colored ribbon among them.

Three dozen hurricane lanterns of various sizes and heights, on different stands or sitting freely on the balcony floor, were arranged among the forest of glittery white trees.

Because the weather was supposed to be absolutely perfect—the only chance of precipitation being some light flurries around midnight, which would be *stunning* for the photographs if it happened—there was no need for the backup plan of a long, narrow tent-like awning that would extend from the door of the tower to the end of the balcony, where the bride and groom would stand.

Callie was ecstatic. She was about to pull off one of the most unique and beautiful winter weddings, with an attractive and very much in love septuagenarian couple, in an infamous location. If everything went well, she'd have spectacular photos for her portfolio, and press coming out the wazoo.

She was on the ground in front of the balcony, checking out the view from below of all angles with the white forest, the hurricane placement, and making certain the greenery swags weren't sagging when she heard a sizzle and a small little explosion.

She looked up to see that the glittery New Year's Eve ball had popped into illumination above the bell tower. Of course, no one could really see the light at ten o'clock in the morning unless they were watching for it. But tonight it would shine and glitter on the twelfth stroke of midnight, and when the ball came on at that time, a small explosion of biodegradable confetti would also rain down on the partygoers.

"Test run looks good!" she called up to Gertie Bachu, the tower's caretaker whom she'd met just this morning.

"All right, thanks," Gertie called down. "Anything else you need checked out?"

"I just want to make sure all the outlets are working on the balcony for the lights on the trees," Callie replied as she turned to go back inside the tower. "I'll check that now."

She'd climbed the fifty stairs to the clock tower room a half dozen times already this morning, so on this—her seventh trip—she decided she could definitely have two pieces of the stunning wedding cake Trib had baked for the happy couple. *And* a champagne cocktail or two—but only after everything went off. Definitely not before.

The room was ready for the caterers, who would set up at eleven fifteen and unveil the food just after the wedding finished—about an hour later. There were standing cocktail tables and a few settees—all in rich velvet upholstery—for the more elderly guests. A freestanding coat rack sat prudently in a corner.

White and cream flowers with green and blue spruce greenery created showy centerpieces on the cocktail tables and the bar. There was a champagne fountain—Iva had insisted, and Hollis had happily paid the price for that extra and for a very fine bubbly—as well as a top-shelf bar.

Callie looked at the wall where Brenda Tremaine's red-painted words had appeared. The message still niggled at her —as any message left by a spiritual hand would no doubt do to most anyone. She and Fiona had washed it off the night of the séance because Iva insisted she didn't want anyone worrying about the curse during her wedding. And Callie and Fiona agreed it would be best if no one knew about the actual séance either.

Farewell, Brenda.

Now, Callie walked back out onto the balcony to check the lighting on the white trees, and to adjust a few of the hurricanes and trees based on what she'd seen from the ground. She was moving one of the trees that was at the front of the balcony when she noticed a black mark on it.

It looked like a scrape, and it hadn't been there—she didn't think—when she put the tree in place. Maybe it had rubbed against the wrought iron railing when she was positioning it.

"No one will see it," she told herself, and left things as they were. When she noticed the same black mark on a couple of the other trees next to the railing, she figured she'd been correct— fresh oil on the railing must have rubbed onto the white paint.

"If that's the least of my worries tonight, it'll be smooth sailing," Callie told herself.

Then she checked the time and realized she could sneak back to Uncle Trib's house for a quick nap.

She'd need it, for it was going to be a late night.

Ben had hoped to see Callie at Tremaine Tower when he stopped by early in the afternoon on New Year's Eve, but he learned she'd already left and wouldn't be back until the bride and groom showed up around eleven pm.

The place looked really nice—especially the elegant white forest of trees on the balcony. The tiny lights would be beautiful at night, and now that he saw the candles he realized he'd always known what a hurricane was—he just didn't know that it had a special name.

He felt a spurt of pride that such a unique and successful event looked ready to go off without a hitch.

Although he'd been looking forward to seeing Callie before the whirlwind of the evening, he was also pleased he was able to access the clock tower room without her being present...because he had one little adjustment to make to the decor.

CHAPTER 11

IVA BERGSTROM WAS the most beautiful bride Callie had ever seen—and that was saying something, as she'd worked on over four hundred weddings during her eight-year career in event planning.

The bride's apple cheeks glowed even more pink and pretty than usual, and her blue eyes sparkled with delight and liveliness—even at eleven o'clock at night when she would normally be sound asleep. She wore a round hat of silvery-white fur just barely tipped with black, and her own silver-white hair curled gently below it.

Two-inch square glittery earrings clung to her ears. Callie was certain the earrings were vintage from the fifties, with rows of baguette-cut crystals positioned in alternating directions...or maybe they were real diamonds; who knew. The bride wore no other jewelry. She didn't need to, for her evening suit dress required no further adornment.

The suit was simple, with smooth lines that nipped in a little at the waist, then followed the same straight fit down over her hips without a peplum. Dramatic lapels made from the same fur as her hat created a shallow vee neckline, but the lapels were long—extending from shoulder to where they narrowed and met at a single sparkling button that matched the earrings, fastened just below the breastbone.

Iva's skirt was floor length, showing just enough of her shoes to reveal the glittery toes that peeped out when she stood for photographs. She wore gloves generously banded with the same fur, and they fit over the wrists of her long, fitted sleeves.

The hat, lapels, and gloves could—if the bride chose—be removed when she went inside for the small reception. But the suit was made from fine wool with a subtle sheen, and would keep her warm while on the balcony.

Hollis Nath, a distinguished-looking and handsome man in his early seventies, wore a classic black tux. His vest and ascot were the same color as his bride's suit, of course, and in deference to the weather, he wore leather gloves and a fine black wool scarf draped over his shoulders. He was hatless. His handsome face was lit with joy, and his cheeks flushed with happiness as well as from the brisk air.

The two had decided against attendants—for a number of reasons, including, Callie was certain, the fact that it would be impossible for Iva to choose bridesmaids from among her Tuesday Ladies and Fiona. Hollis's beloved grandson Gideon —who was Fiona's serious boyfriend—had been fine with not being a groomsman while his grandfather married the love of his life.

"That way I can keep my own future bride warm," he teased Fiona—who claimed she was allergic to commitment.

She looked up at him with a teasing grin. "We'll talk!"

The bride and groom stood on the balcony, looking down

at the hundred or so people who'd gathered below. They chatted and called down to their friends from their twenty-foot-high perch. Most of the crowd were invited guests, but there were others who'd come to the square to count down to midnight and watch the ball light up.

The area below the balcony, along with several walk-ways, had been cleared of snow. Five different fire pits had been arranged in the area, and they blazed with welcome heat. The caterers walked around with s'mores prepared on wooden skewers, inviting the guests to toast them on the fire pits. They also offered hot chocolate, tea, and coffee—spiked or unspiked.

Maxine and Juanita had camped out in front of the fire pit closest to the balcony. Bruce Banner was dressed in a thick sweater that looked like a tuxedo, and he wore a jaunty white tie on his collar. Standing next to them was Doc Horner, the town veterinarian and the object of Juanita's marital interest for over a decade. Perhaps she was hoping the idea of the wedding would rub off on him, Callie thought. Orbra and her trucker husband (who happened to be in town for once) stood next to them, along with the poor server whom Maxine had banned from leaving their proximity until the tray of s'mores needed to be refilled.

Maxine was currently badgering a different server—who held a tray of drinks—to add extra Bailey's to her next hot chocolate.

Cherry and William Reckless—who was her high school flame, a tall, lean man who'd just returned from seven years in Tibet—wandered over to say hi to Bruce Banner and the others. They were holding steaming drinks of Orbra's Honey-bear Hot Toddy—tea spiked with whiskey and a syrup made from orange peel, honey, and sage. Callie could identify the drink from a distance due to the orange garnish perched on the cup rim and she nodded to herself. That was her favorite of the hot beverage offerings tonight.

Fiona and Gideon stood near a different roaring fire, and were joined by Declan, the blacksmith, and Leslie Nakano, whom Callie knew owned the Shenstone House bed and breakfast—with its hidden speakeasy—up on the hill. They were chatting with another couple whom Callie hadn't met, but she knew the pretty blond woman was the owner of the stage theater in town and her date was a doctor who made fresh bread in his spare time[1]. Her heart skipped a little beat when she noticed Ben Tremaine standing there too, and she watched for a moment to see whether he'd brought a date.

Not that it mattered. He'd already made it clear that he wasn't interested in anything more than friendship.

But still...it was New Year's Eve, and she simply couldn't help remembering what happened sixteen years ago. Like it or not, it was an anniversary of sorts.

The clock struck eleven-thirty, and despite the disappointment of her unrequited crush, Callie was filled with her own burst of energy and pleasure.

Everything was going just perfectly. She'd been on and off the balcony, up and down the stairs (she'd change into heels for the reception later; but for now, she wore comfortable, warm shoes), checked on the caterers (not that they needed checking as they were Trib's), and now she would head back inside to be there before the ceremony began.

She paused to speak to one of the servers, then said hi to Maxine, Juanita, and company. She told herself she was only doing her job when she stopped at the cluster of people with

Fiona, Gideon, Ben, and the others. She was proud of herself when her greeting to Ben was warm and casual, and even accepted a friendly hug from him as he congratulated her on a beautiful event.

Dang, he smelled *good*. A little smoky from the fire, a little wintry from the air, and something else that was fresh and clean and *yummy*.

She extricated herself reluctantly and had a few more words with Fiona—and met the stage theater owner, Vivien Savage, and the bread-making doctor, Jake DeRiccio.

When Baxter approached, camera in hand for the story he was doing for the local papers, she gratefully excused herself to speak with him.

Then she realized it was eleven forty-five and she needed to get upstairs! Fifteen minutes until the clock began to strike, and about eighteen minutes until the actual vows were to be exchanged.

She hurried away and climbed up the stairs once more. She'd done it often enough her butt should be getting tighter, but sadly, she didn't think that was the case. Still, she made it up in less than five minutes and let herself into the room.

All right. Here we go.

She started to walk toward the door of the balcony, intending to hover just at the back and out of sight as the clock striking and ceremony proceeded, just in case she was needed.

But something stopped her. Something in the air...something shifting and cool and—

"Oh no you *don't*," she hissed, looking around the room. "No, Brenda, *no*, please...not tonight. Please!"

But the air was definitely moving, beginning to swirl, and

Callie began to panic. Her palms went damp and her stomach began to cringe and twist frighteningly. She couldn't get sick now, she had to stop this, she had to—

"*Ware...*

"*Rail...*"

Callie froze. She could *feel* rather than hear the words... just as had happened before. Brenda had communicated with her this way once before—crying "*Nooooo!*" when Callie had first visited her—and now, for some reason, she was speaking again.

Well, of course she knew the reason—the crazy ghost wanted to ruin Iva and Hollis's wedding!

"*WARE... RAIL... !*"

"What are you saying? What are you talking about?" Callie walked up to the portrait of Brenda, her heart pounding, her stomach in knots even as the air began to ruffle and whip more violently at her. "I don't understand why you can't just leave—"

Callie jumped when the clock began to strike and she started toward the door that led to the balcony.

She had to be out there to make sure everything went all right. She didn't have time to deal with a freaky ghost.

She had to make sure everything went as planned: that the clock struck, the bells rang, the ball of light exploded—

Exploded.

Callie stopped, her hand on the doorknob.

Black marks on the white trees.

Ware... rail.

Black marks... *scorch* marks?

Scorch marks!

It hit her, all at once, what Brenda had been trying to say—and what had happened, somehow—all those years ago.

The clock was still striking, but in only a few moments, on the last bong, the glittery ball would burst into light—

Callie burst through the door onto the the balcony, screaming as she ran outside.

"Don't touch the railing!"

---

1. *Sinister Stage*

CHAPTER 12

"THANK GOD YOU FIGURED IT OUT," Fiona was saying. "You saved their lives!"

She was about the fiftieth person to do so—to say those words, to hug Callie with relief, to pull back and look over at the happy—and alive—bride and groom.

It was after one o'clock, and because the bride and groom were in their seventies—as were most of their friends—everything was winding down.

"I almost didn't," Callie replied, then, unlike with most of the others who'd thanked her, she spilled more details to Fiona. "But Brenda came back and she was really insistent, and I tried to ignore her, to beg her to leave...and then it struck me. The deaths only happened on New Year's Eve—and the only thing that happened differently on New Year's Eve was *when the ball lit up.*

"I had been here earlier today when Gertie was testing the ball, and I noticed black marks on the trees that were standing right up against the wrought iron railing. I thought it was oil from the railing, but I realized at that moment—just in time—that they were scorch marks."

"And you put two and two together in about ten seconds," said Gideon, who still looked tense about everything even though no one had died. "Thank God."

Callie nodded, still trying to swallow the lump in her throat that had been there for over an hour. "Yes. I guess—I mean, we'll have to confirm it—but I think there's probably some exposed wire that touches the railing, and when the electricity is sent up to the ball to light up, it zaps through the railing. If you're touching it, you're..." She swallowed again, hard, and realized how close things had come to being a tragedy. "Toast."

"So it's not really a curse after all," said Fiona. "It's just a faulty wiring job."

"That's right," said Gideon, who wasn't one to openly discuss curses or phantoms. "Just a simple, scientific explanation."

"But you have to wonder whether Lonna Donne had something to do with it originally," mused Callie. "For all we know, she somehow planned it as her revenge."

"We'll probably never know the truth about that, but I can promise that tomorrow Gertie will check everything over with a fine tooth comb," said a familiar voice.

Callie turned to find Ben standing there. The way he was looking at her made her stomach do a slow, pleasant roll. "You were brilliant," he said. "Brilliant to figure that out. Amazing job, Callie. On the wedding and everything."

Her face felt very warm and she wasn't sure what to think about this sudden *look* from him. She'd been wrong before... "Thank you, Ben. I—"

He was still eyeing her, but his words were benign. "I... uh...as a member of the Tremaines, I want to thank you for settling the so-called curse legend once and for all."

"Well, I'm really happy to have figured it out. Otherwise...." She shuddered and grimaced. "I almost didn't. I keep thinking about it..."

"It's over. And everything went perfectly. The ceremony was just what you planned—just what you'd described to me. I really liked that tea drink with the whiskey they were serving down there—and I'm not a tea drinker. And the s'mores...that was a great idea too! This has been a *wonderful* New Year's Eve."

She realized that somehow as they were talking, they'd edged away from the main crowd of people and were standing kind of alone, off to the side. "Thank you, Ben, it really means..."

She stopped because he was looking up.

She tilted her head to follow his gaze and then she saw it.

A ball of mistletoe...right above her head.

It was new. Brand new. And *she* hadn't put it there.

She looked back at him, suddenly feeling very warm and very tingly. Her stomach rolled again, extremely pleasantly.

Ben wore a little smirk behind his beard, but there was question in his eyes. "Ooops," he said with fake surprise. "Look where you're standing."

"I see that." Warmth and joy flowed through her as she became certain. Well, *pretty* certain... She couldn't tamp back a grin. "Oh dear, whatever shall I d—"

Her words were cut off as he stepped close, pulled her to him, and covered her mouth with his. Heat, pleasure, and relief coursed through her as she met his kiss eagerly.

So right.

So perfect, so right, so *damned* long coming. His beard bristled softly against her face, his arms held her close, and they kissed with emotions that had been pent-up for over sixteen years.

When at last Callie pulled back—just to catch her breath —she had to touch his face. "Did you...when did you...?" She could barely form words, but she could look up meaningfully at the mistletoe.

"Earlier today," he replied. His voice was low and rough and she liked that she'd made him sound like that. "I couldn't let another New Year's Eve go by without picking up where we left off...sixteen years ago."

"It's about damned time," she muttered, and pulled him back for another long kiss.

He was the one to ease away the next time. "So, uh...how much longer do you have to hang around here?"

She glanced around, saw that the caterers were doing their job of cleaning up, and grinned up at him as she settled her hips against his. *Oh my.* He was definitely very happy to see her.

"Not long...why do you ask?"

"Because I've got a fire ready to go at my house, and I'd really like to see you naked in the firelight. As soon as possible."

The bottom dropped out of her belly and Callie felt like she was about to spontaneously combust from the look he was giving her. She managed to form the words: "Give me ten minutes."

As she walked away, she heard him say, "Only ten minutes *and sixteen years.*"

CHAPTER 13

"WHEN YOU STOKE A FIRE, you really stoke a fire," Callie murmured, sliding a hand over Ben's bare chest. "That blaze went on all night."

And so had they.

They'd had, as Ben had said, sixteen years to make up for.

He gave her a loud smack of a kiss on her cheek—which was more than a little raw from lots of beard scratches—and slid from the bed. He stretched and scratched his beard, then his chest, and glanced at the clock—which read a little after ten. "Want some coffee?"

"Yes, please," she replied, snuggling back under the covers that were still warm from his body heat. She was, after all, quite naked.

She was just beginning to slip back into a very satisfied slumber when she heard a wordless exclamation from Ben, somewhere out in the rest of the house.

"What is it?" she called.

There was a pause, then he replied, "You made the front page."

"I did? Oh, fantastic!" Callie bounced upright in bed, tucking the pillow behind her back and the blankets over her breasts. She'd been so pleased with how Iva and Hollis's wedding had gone—and that she and Ben had finally moved from friends to lovers—that she'd almost forgotten about her hopes for some good press to go along with her stress-inducing marketing tactic. "Do you have the paper? Or is it online?"

He came into the bedroom. He carried the *Wicks Hollow Gazette* and two cups of coffee, and was wearing a strange expression. As if he were trying to keep a straight face.

"Both, probably." He tossed the paper to her and Callie flipped it open to the front page.

"Oh my *God!*" She stared at the large, full-color photograph that took up two thirds of the page.

It was a beautiful picture of the bride and groom standing at the railing of the balcony. The huge clock face above their heads showed less than one tick mark between 11:59 and midnight. The white forest of trees and the candles surrounded them, creating a fairy-tale like scene. It was stunning...

Except for the wild, wide-eyed, open-mouthed Callie bursting through the doorway behind them. She was caught in mid-leap and mid-scream, her arms flailing, her bright red hair a wild splash of color in the exact center of the photograph, her face positioned precisely between Iva's and Hollis's.

The headline read: **NYE CURSE CURED**

"I'm going to *kill* Baxter for this," she said, starting to giggle as she stared at the terrible, awful, hilariously ridiculous photograph. "He just *had* to use that photo! Forget the curse—I'm going to murder him!"

But she couldn't control her laughter. It was just so ludicrous, and she was so relieved the wedding was over, that no one had died, and that she was here, with Ben Tremaine, at last.

He was laughing too, and he leaned over to gather her into a great big hug. "I was afraid you'd be upset," he said.

By now she'd lost control of herself and was laughing so hard she decided she'd better get out of bed before she peed herself—and the sheets. "Only me," she gasped, dragging herself out of bed, weak with laughter. "Only I would turn a brilliant marketing scheme into a circus."

He looked at her, his eyes so dark and serious. "And that's what I love about you, Callie—one of the things I've always loved about you: that you can find the humor in even the seemingly worst situations."

She stopped laughing. Her heart stopped beating for an instant, then swelled with happiness. "Oh Ben, I've waited such a long time to hear you say something like that."

"I've waited longer to say it," he replied. "And I just have one request from you, Callie Quigley."

"What's that?" She stood at the edge of the bed, looking down at him—no longer laughing because of the very serious look in his eyes.

"Actually, two requests," he said, taking her hand in his.

"All right. What are they?"

"First, that the next wedding you plan will be ours," he said—and she squeaked out a gasp.

"Are you serious?"

"Well, when you realize you want to spend the rest of

your life with someone..." he began, quoting her favorite movie.

"You want the rest of your life to start as soon as possible," she replied, giving his beard an affectionate tug. "I know the feeling." She leaned forward to kiss him, and he dragged her back onto the bed.

A few moments later, she pulled away from a very hot kiss, and some other very hot activity, and said, "Wait...what was the other thing?"

He grinned at her. "That we get married *after* April 15th. Tax Day. Because I want a *very* long honeymoon."

She burst out laughing and shook her head. "It'll have to be after wedding season then—like in January."

"A year from now, January? I am not waiting that long—"

"You waited sixteen years already," she teased.

"Longer than that. How about we get married next week?"

"Next *week?*"

"It's before tax season ramps up and after wedding season. It's perfect."

"But—"

"And you're a wedding planner. You know how to make it happen."

She looked at him and realized he was absolutely serious. "Well," she replied, feeling a little unsteady but ecstatic nonetheless. "I think that's something we can negotiate."

"I'm good at negotiating. Let's start *now.*" He was about to dive under the covers when he paused. And then a wicked, oh, so wicked grin spread over his face. "I have an idea...let's play Trivial Pursuit. My nieces and nephews gave me the Harry Potter deluxe version for Christmas."

And that was how Callie ended up putting six articles of clothing *back* on...only to take them off again when Ben Tremaine, the Trivia King, handily won the game...

But in the end, Callie figured she ended up being the *real* winner...sixteen years and one cured curse later.

ORBRA'S HONEYBEAR HOT TODDY
RECIPE

Make this fabulous syrup and add to whiskey and/or tea (or both, as Orbra says!) and enjoy a wonderful winter drink.

INGREDIENTS

- Peels from 2-3 *washed* oranges
- 1 cup of honey*
- 1/4 cup brown sugar (or regular sugar)

- 10-15 large, fresh sage leaves; include the stems if you like

DIRECTIONS

- (Optional: Roast the orange peels in the oven by putting them on a cookie sheet at 400° F for about ten-fifteen minutes; until they turn a little brown and become fragrant.)
- Add all ingredients, plus 1.5 cups of water, to a saucepan.
- Bring to a boil, stirring occasionally.
- Once boiling, turn heat down to simmer. Stir occasionally. It's okay if the syrup foams up a little; just stir it back in.
- After about 20-30 minutes, your syrup is finished. Taste it. It should be very, very sweet. And yummy!
- Remove the orange peels and sage, and strain the rest of the syrup into a container (glass is best).
- You can refrigerate the syrup in a covered container for two weeks...although I doubt it'll last that long.
- Makes about 1.5 cups of syrup.
- Add to hot tea or whiskey (or both!) to taste. I usually do about one part syrup to two parts whiskey, but I like this particular drink sweet. 😊
- Please note: the syrup won't be really thick.
- Garnish with orange slices or orange peels that you've cut into strips and roasted in the oven. (Not the ones you used for the syrup.)

❄

* Honey can be expensive, so here are a couple of
options:
1. Split the cup of honey between honey and regular
granulated sugar (1/2 and 1/2 or whatever combination you want. Best results will include at least a half
cup of honey).
2. Buy honey from discount stores like HomeGoods
or dollar stores—honey never spoils, and you're going
to be cooking with it, so why not?

ENJOY! And let me know if you liked the recipe and what
you did with it.

BONUS: IN WHICH MISS GARDELLA RECEIVES THREE GIFTS

A VERY SHORT INCIDENT IN THE LIFE OF VICTORIA GARDELLA

This is a very short story that would have taken place around Christmastime during the first book in my Gardella series, The Rest Falls Away. This story originally appeared in a holiday collection called "Tiny Treats."

London, 1819

Miss Victoria Gardella Grantworth was an unusual woman by the standards of London Society, commonly known as the *ton*. Although she was quite beautiful—with thick, dark, unruly hair and intelligent hazel eyes, and appeared no different than the other young women who'd debuted into Society during the current Season—she did, in fact, have a secret.

She was a vampire hunter—one from the long line of the Gardella family—and had just recently learned of her duty to carry the stake. She knew what it was like to shove a sharp, pointed piece of wood into the heart of a red-eyed man who was about to plunge his fangs into her—or someone else's —neck.

Other than the poof of foul-smelling ash, however, once the stake was slammed into the creature's heart, the incident was over...and most often, Victoria found herself rejoining whatever festivity or event in which she'd previously been participating before being called away to attend to her duty. A ball at Almack's, a theatrical play the Drury Lane theater, a moonlight walk through Vauxhall Gardens, a musicale in the stuffy parlor room of an acquaintance. Of course, there were times when she might return with a torn dress, oozing vampire bites, or other mishaps...but that was part of her life.

It was her responsibility to keep Londoners safe.

If she had the occasional nightmare about red-eyed demonic men tearing into her throat, or sharp-fanged women clawing violently into her flesh, it was to be expected. She'd faced those incidents more than once...and had kept a number of young women and handsome dandies from being mauled into a bloody pulp.

But tonight was Christmas Eve, and tonight hunting and slaying vampires was as far from Victoria's mind as it could ever be—which was to say, not completely gone, but certainly not at the forefront of her thoughts.

Lady Melly Grantworth, Victoria's mother, came bustling down the stairs, giving orders and opinions to all and sundry as usual. "Victoria, be certain to take your blue cloak. The snow is coming down quite thickly, and it is more than a bit chilly. The wind is whipping up! Parsons, the coach must be brought around and warm bricks put in there immediately. The church is two blocks away, and then after we will attend the Christmas Eve dinner at Duchess Farnley's."

Lady Melly paused at the bottom of the stairs. "What's this?"

Victoria turned, in the process of donning the brilliant blue cape lined with rabbit fur, and saw three packages sitting on the foyer table.

"I do believe they are for you, Victoria," her mother said. There was a combination of suspicion and delight in her eyes —for even from where she stood, Victoria could see the wax seal on one of them that clearly belonged to one of the peerage. More than anything, Lady Melly wanted her daughter to wed—and to wed for money and power.

But of course, a vampire hunter simply could not marry. Especially a female one. Thus, Melly was going to have a great disappointment in her life.

"They're for me? Three packages?" Victoria paused in donning her gloves—not her favorite ones, unfortunately, for she'd recently lost one in the dangerous neighborhood of St. Giles. (A place a normal woman of the *ton* would never dare visit.)

"They certainly appear to be. Look at them."

"How interesting," Victoria murmured as she examined them, and a little prickle of knowing trickled over her shoulders. "How curious."

The first one, a perfectly square box, was tied with an ornate bow. The box itself had been covered with glitter, and it sparkled in the low light of the foyer. It was the heaviest of the three, and the most beautiful. There was a small notecard with the seal of the Marquess of Rockley (the most eligible bachelor of the *ton*) and her name was written in formal penmanship: *Miss Grantworth.*

Victoria untied the bow, tucking the glittering silver fabric away to be used for trim later, and opened the box. Melly, who'd been hovering over her shoulder, gasped when she saw the glittering jewels inside.

"Why, that's worth a small fortune, Victoria!" her mother squealed. "Rockley has indeed set his cap for you!" She fairly began to dance around the foyer.

Victoria lifted the necklet of golden-topaz gems from its mooring. It glowed and glittered, the jewels catching the light like a soft fire. "It's beautiful," she murmured, thinking of how handsome and charming and dashing Lord Rockley was. They had shared several dances over the last weeks, and he had made his interest clear. And she could not deny that her own heart beat much more quickly when in his presence. He'd even kissed her during a ride in the park.

"You must change your gown, Victoria," Melly ordered. "So you can wear them tonight! Rockley will be at the dinner, and he will want to see you in those jewels."

But Victoria shook her head. "I don't have the time to change, Mother. Perhaps tomorrow night." And she picked up the second package.

It was long and flat, and very light. While not wrapped as prettily as the one from Rockley, this gift was packaged in pale pink paper. A dried rose with small touches of real boxwood were tied in place with gold lace, making the gift appear both elegant and understated. The card simply said *Victoria* in a simple, masculine hand.

"Who on earth—" Melly said, hovering once more.

Victoria didn't have an answer until she pulled the golden lace free and opened the flat box. Nestled inside, wrapped in clove-scented tissue paper, was a pair of gloves. They were exquisitely tailored of supple ivory calfskin, with delicate stitching and tasteful embellishments. Only one person she knew would have such excellent taste.

A flush rushed up over Victoria's cheeks as she pulled the pair free and a small note fluttered to the floor. *Perhaps you should have a complete set,* was all it said—but she had already realized the giver.

Sebastian Vioget, disreputable, mysterious, and as handsome as a golden god, had boldly and impolitely relieved her of one of her gloves during their first meeting...and had refused to give it back. His golden-amber eyes had been hot and filled with promise as he stripped the glove from her hand and then leaned in to kiss her.

"Victoria! What on earth is wrong with you? Are you catching a fever? Your cheeks are *red.*"

She looked at her mother, and the flush dissipated. "No, not at all."

"And who are those gloves from? They are very expensive. Surely you don't have *two* suitors! Why, you cannot do anything to jeopardize your arrangement with Rockley!" Melly screeched. "You cannot wear those tonight. They don't match your gown!"

"No, of course not, Mother," Victoria said mildly. She'd learned long ago to just let her mother prattle on—and then to do whatever she wanted to do. She tucked the gloves away to be worn another time.

"What on earth is *this* one?" Melly was examining the third present—which could hardly be considered a gift at all. It certainly didn't look like one. "It looks as if a beggar wrapped it up for you, Victoria. Why on earth would a beggar give you a gift? "

Just as intrigued, she took up the last item. Long, slender, and thin, the package was loosely wrapped with plain brown paper and tied with twine. Her name had been written directly on the paper in an impatient dark scrawl: *V. Gardella.*

She immediately knew who'd sent it. For some reason, she felt it necessary to turn away from Lady Melly when opening it—which was fine, for her mother had gone back to ogling the topaz necklace.

After she tore the paper away, Victoria found herself holding a lethal-looking stake. Made from ash—the most potent of wood for annihilating the undead—it was carved into a long, smooth weapon. The point had been painted with silver, except for the very tip of the sharp wood—which was left naked so that the ash would come into direct contact with the undead's demonic heart. A cross of silver had been stamped into the flat end of the stake, and the weapon itself was painted a sleek black.

From Max Pesaro, of course. The most powerful Venator —vampire hunter—Victoria knew. Her colleague and nemesis, and a man who didn't believe a woman could be a vampire hunter.

As one might expect, there was no note—but his message was clear as if it had been written: *Forget the fripperies, the flirtations, and the jewels. This is your life.*

Victoria looked at the stake—beautiful in its own right, she had to admit—and a welling of frustration, determination, and then acceptance flooded her. He was right. This was her life.

"Victoria, we really *must* go!" Melly demanded.

Very well, then. She would go.

Victoria looked at the gifts—the jewels, the gloves, the stake.

Only one of them would accompany her tonight.

The one that mattered.

If you'd like to read more about Victoria Gardella and her adventures in 19th Century London as a woman trying to balance her life—and society's expectations (not to mention her mother's!)—while trying to save the world, you can download *The Rest Falls Away* for ***free*** from most retailers (Amazon, Apple, Nook, Kobo, GooglePlay).

Or you can click here to download to your ereader immediately.

WHAT ARE YOU DOING NEW YEAR'S EVE?

When you turn the page, you'll find a short novel that appeared in the anthology *Countdown to a Kiss*, which I wrote with three other of my closest writer friends. All of the stories take place on New Year's Eve, and since mine is the first you can consider it a teaser to whet your whistle!

Countdown to a Kiss is available wherever ebooks are sold —and there are print versions as well.

A little note about some of the characters in the story...

Helen Galliday is the inspiration for Maxine Took, of the Wicks Hollow series. I tried to figure out a way to simply lift Tess's Aunt Helen from Henderson, North Carolina, and bring her to Wicks Hollow, but it simply didn't work. So just consider that Maxine as her soul sister. 😉

And second, Johnny Wilder is, in my mind, the nephew of Cherry Wilder—the yoga teacher in Wicks Hollow...

because *all* of my stories exist in the same universe (although sometimes alternate realities).

I hope you enjoy the read!

— Colleen Gleason
December 2020

CHAPTER 1

NEW YEAR'S EVE: Present Day

"I am *not* going to kiss Lewis Kampmueller at midnight."

Tess Devine glared at herself in the rearview mirror of her BMW, practicing for the firm refusal she was going to give her sisters tonight. Then she realized the traffic light had turned green and she returned her attention to the road, accelerating smoothly out of the parking lot of Henderson Community Hospital.

She waved to Mrs. Linkline, giving a little toot of the horn, as she cruised toward downtown Henderson, which was all decked out in cheery holiday decor. Mrs. L, her old Algebra and Geometry teacher, waved back and made motions that clearly said *See you tonight!*

Right. See you tonight.

No way am I going stag to the party. And no way am I going to kiss Lewis.

For the last decade, Tess and her younger sisters had lied,

cheated, dodged and otherwise manipulated each other, determined not to be the one in their family to kiss Lewis at midnight.

And if the confident, flamboyant, never-without-a-date, semi-famous Tess Devine actually had to finally kiss the geekiest guy in town, Grace and Annabelle would never let her hear the end of it. Hell, it would probably end up as a sidebar on Page Six or on one of the gossip sites: *Broadway Star goes Stag to Own Family's New Year's Eve Bash/Forced to Kiss Sisters' Reject.*

Someone would probably even post a picture on Facebook.

Her sisters would especially love it, for in the decade since they'd first made the bet, Tess made sure she never had to kiss Lewis. It was usually poor Grace who'd had to kiss him...not that he minded at all. Anyone with a pair of eyes in their head knew he'd been in love with the middle Devine sister since he was sixteen. And Tess figured it was her job as matchmaker and older sister to help facilitate True Love.

Tess grinned at her reflection, remembering how nearly every year, Lewis—sometimes with her help or Annabelle's—made sure poor Gracie would be left high and dry without a date at midnight. No matter how hard the middle sister tried, her escort never lasted until the witching hour—if he even made it to the party in the first place.

Poor Lewis. If he didn't close the deal this year, he was just going to have to give up. What the hell was wrong with the guy?

Just then she heard the perky tones of *Bibbidi-Bobbidi-Boo* coming from the depths of her purse. Speak of the devil.

She pushed her Bluetooth earpiece and answered the

call. "Hey Grace." Her sister—an FBI Special Agent—would never know she'd picked such a fluffy song for her special ringtone. If Grace ever found out, she'd probably do one of her FBI moves on Tess and break her neck. (Although Grace always denied having any lethal moves, Tess didn't believe her.)

"Are you almost here? I can't wait to see you!"

"About fifteen more minutes. Had to stop at Birdie's and then the hospital to visit some of the children," Tess replied. "And I know why you want to see me so badly—because you haven't picked out anything to wear yet, have you?"

"Nooo," moaned Grace. "Belly's going to have my head. Can't you get here any sooner? I have to have something before she gets here. She sent me links four months ago. And then another month later. And she tried to set me up with a damned personal shopper. What the hell am I going to do with a personal fucking shopper? Have you heard from her?"

Tess was laughing. Poor Grace. If she had her way, she'd throw on a black t-shirt and a pair of dress slacks for the party, not caring that everyone else would be in tuxes and evening gowns. "No—but she's supposed to be en route from Raleigh."

"I've been trying to catch her on her cell for the last hour, and all I get is voicemail."

"You know her—she's probably dictating seating charts or picking out a dress...for next year's party. I wonder who she'll bring this year for her date," Tess said hopefully. If Annabelle didn't have a date either, their agreement dictated they would both have to kiss Lewis.

"I don't know—but you can bet she'll bring someone. She

swore to me she wasn't going to be stuck with Lewis this year."

"How about you? Who's going to be on your arm?"

"A big bad wolf, as a matter of fact," Grace said mysteriously. "What about you, big sister dear? Now that you're single again...."

Tess laughed, hardly even feeling the pang of pain and shame thanks to her pending divorce. "I'm not telling. You'll have to wait and see." After all, there was still hope. Maybe the bartender would be cute. "Well, I've got to run. I'll see you in a few."

As she ended the call, Tess braked in front of Clavell's Pharmacy to let a woman and her two children cross, then stuck her head out the window when she recognized her. "Hey, Deanne! You're coming tonight, right?"

The woman waved and brought her children over to the car, ignoring the light but steady traffic going through the quaint downtown. "Hi Tess! You know I wouldn't miss it for the world. Joey and I look forward to it every year—well, at least I do. Joey would rather not be stuffed into a tux, but he knows he'll have fun anyway."

"I can't wait to see your dress," Tess said. "You always wear something fabulous. Did you get great shoes?"

"Oh yes—Annabelle sent me a link to a great online shoe place and I found the perfect pair. Wait till you see them!"

"Make sure you get there early," Tess told her. "And park in the side lot—it's easier to get in that way. The band is going to be great, so don't forget to bring your socks so you can take off your shoes!"

One of Deanne's children, Dusty, tugged on her mom's hand. Deanne bent to her and said, "Say hi to Miss Tess. Do you remember her? She was Belle when we went to see *Beauty and the Beast.* Remember, when we visited Auntie Susan in New York?"

Tess smiled at Dusty and her younger brother Joe Junior. "I remember you—you came to visit me backstage after the show. I showed you the glass with the rose inside it, remember?" The little girl was cute as a button, with just the right amount of freckles on her pug nose. Tess tightened her insides against an envious pang.

"You don't look like Belle," Dusty said, shielding her eyes from the noon December sun. "She had hair...." She moved her hand in a gesture that clearly indicated Tess's long honey blonde hair was not the same as Belle's brown, elegant updo.

"That's because I wore a wig. See?" Tess snatched up the Belle wig, which she'd tossed on the seat next to her, and was now muddled up with the familiar yellow dress. She still wore that costume to visit children in the hospital, for they never tired of Belle.

A gentle toot behind them made Deanne and Tess look around. "Guess we'd better move," Dee said. "See you tonight!" And she hurried off with her two munchkins.

Dee's parting words brought her thoughts back to the problem at hand. Because...really. Tess Devine could *not* go to the biggest shindig in Henderson without a date. Hmm. Maybe she could just pretend she was still married....No. She didn't want to be attached to Barry any longer.

Whatever. I'm not going to kiss Lewis, no matter how hard Grace and Belly try. I'm almost twenty-nine years old. I've been nominated for a Tony. I've been on the cover of Fashion. *I've been on a date with Matthew Morrison.*

If I can handle a drunk co-star feeling me up live onstage, I can handle my sisters.

Especially since the drunken co-star had been a woman.

Lewis wasn't that bad—not anymore, anyway. Sure, he'd been a four-eyed gweeb with his face always in a computer back in high school, but the biggest problem with him hadn't been that as much as Mom and Dad. They'd had some medieval fantasy about joining the Devine and Kampmueller families for twenty years, and all three of the Devine sisters had rebelled against the idea of a forced marriage, so to speak. Poor Lewis wasn't so much a nerd as he was The Guy Your Mom Wanted You To Marry, So of Course You Didn't.

"Hell, maybe I should just give it up and kiss Lewis this year," Tess said aloud as she drove by the massive Christmas tree at the center of town. It always reminded her of the one in *How the Grinch Stole Christmas*. "Then I'll have had my turn and we can put this stupid game to rest. Ten years is enough."

I wonder if Johnny Wilder's in town....

A hot little shiver caught her by surprise when she thought of seeing Wilder. They used to be friends and had usually ended up hanging out in some form or another on New Year's Eve. Then things had changed.

It had been four years since that awkward night. They'd both had too much to drink and it was late and the things that had been said...well, she doubted he even remembered them. *Surely* he didn't remember them.

Besides. She was no fool. He'd just been trying to get in her pants, just like he did with every other female he encountered. Johnny Wilder was a Player—definitely with a capital P—and that was the last thing she needed in her life right now. She was turning over a new leaf, starting a new phase... and she didn't need a guy like him to screw it up.

What she needed was someone safe and easy.

Which meant she needed to work on Plan B...and quickly. Because she was pulling in the driveway now. After she parked, she pulled out her phone and, grinning, sent a text to Lewis Kampmueller: *Find me a date or you're kissing me tonight, hot stuff.*

That ought to light a fire under his butt.

CHAPTER 2

JOHNNY WILDER FOUND it damn near impossible not to think about Tess Devine on New Year's Eve.

He supposed it was to be expected. After all, she'd pretty much fubarred every one of the last ten of them for him. Even the ones when they hadn't been on the same continent.

He hadn't seen her in four years—three of which had been spent nearly getting his ass blown up in Iraq. And the fourth he'd been safely down at NASA. Not hiding so much as...avoiding.

So here he sat, nursing an IPA in a tall, brown bottle and watching whatever was on ESPN, trying to forget it was New Year's Eve. Trying to forget the Curse of Tess Devine. He was determined that his date Laney would break the tradition tonight, because his track record was pathetic.

And the pisser of it was every damn time he heard "What Are You Doing New Year's Eve?"—which seemed to be the frigging favorite song of every female he'd ever known, not to mention on the soundtrack at every damned store or restaurant he stepped foot in—all he could think of was Tess.

Because, whether he'd intended it or not, she was *his* New Year's Eve tradition.

The sharp click of heels caught his attention as his mom walked in from the garage via the kitchen.

"Back already?" he asked, craning to look behind him as she came into the living room.

"It's so cold out there," Mom said, taking off a thick scarf and gloves. "I can't remember the last time it was this cold in Henderson. They're even calling for snow tonight—which I don't believe for a minute."

"So how's Rhapsody today? Did she spit up? Fart? Fill her diaper?" He grinned up at her as she stopped and gave his too-long hair an affectionate yank.

"My only grandchild is a brilliant baby. She does everything right even though she's only three weeks old."

At twenty-seven, he was a commercial pilot, had completed two tours in Iraq—and seen things he needed to forget—plus knew how to navigate a space shuttle...yet his mom's affectionate touch made him feel all of ten again. Warm and comfortable. Come to think of it, it was probably the same for her. She hadn't seen enough of her only son for four years—a fact which she constantly reminded him.

"Not sure how so much brilliance can happen with a name like *Rhapsody*." Wilder laughed when his mom winced. He still couldn't believe Karen and Mark had named their daughter after a defunct online music service, and he had a feeling his mom felt the same way—though she'd sure as hell never admit it.

She knuckled down on his head, mussing harder, then plopped on the couch next to him. "Are you sure you don't want to get this mop cut before the soirée tonight? I'm sure

Birdie could still fit you in. In fact, I'll make sure of it." She pulled out her cell phone.

"I had it buzzed for four years. I like it longer. All the better for some hot chick to run her fingers through," he teased, lifting his beer to take a drink.

She rolled her eyes and filched the beer from his fingers. "Laney Boudreau better behave with my only son tonight," she warned, then took a sip.

"Rick Stanick better behave with my only mom tonight," he retorted.

His parents had divorced five years ago—just before he joined the Air Force. And then he had to go and get shipped to Iraq a year later and give his mom something else to stress about. Great job, Wilder.

Which was the only reason he was spending the holidays back here in Henderson—to make up for that.

"Oh, you'll never guess who I ran into at Birdie's today," she said, handing him back the beer. "By the way, ugh." She nodded at the bottle. "Too bitter for me."

"I'm sure Rick will bring you a nice bottle of cabernet tonight," he teased.

"He does have excellent taste in wine. And women. Speaking of which, John—you didn't even say anything about my hair. What do you think?"

"Huh? Oh, it looks *great*, Mom." She'd left four hours ago, and as far as he could tell, nothing had changed. "The color's really nice," he said, picking one of the two options he knew was available—color or length. He figured he had a fifty/fifty chance.

"You did notice," she said with a surprised smile. "I guess they taught you something in the service. Well, enjoy your—

whatever you're watching. I've got to start getting ready. Takes me nearly ten minutes just to squeeze into my Spanx, plus all the other stuff we women have to do."

He had no idea what spanks was—but it sounded like something he didn't want to know. The idea of his mom dating (and presumably having sex) was still a little awkward, and spanks sounded vaguely dirty. Definitely something he didn't want to know about. "Okay."

She started to leave then stopped. "Oh yes, I didn't tell you who I ran into at the salon. Tess Devine. Apparently she's in town after all. All the ladies at Birdie's were a-twitter —ha!" —she poked him— "because she came in to show them some wigs and hairpieces they're using in *Wicked*. Did you know they have over a hundred and fifty of them in all?"

But he wasn't listening anymore. He'd stopped after *she's in town after all.*

No frigging *way*.

How the hell did that happen?

"Rick should be here in about two hours. Remember your Southern manners, Johnny-boy," she said, and laid a loud kiss on his cheek. "And if you leave before I see you, make sure you save a dance for me tonight."

"I will," he said weakly, wondering how much of a chance he'd have of sweet-talking Laney into staying home in the hot tub instead of going to the Devine-Kampmueller shindig. It'd be a lot more fun trying to peel her out of a red dress than making small talk with Tess Devine and her asshat of a husband.

Probably a snowball's chance in hell. The soirée, as his mom called it, was the biggest to-do in Henderson, and everyone who was in town attended. It was a damned tradition. Which was why he'd made certain Tess Devine was still doing her stint in *Wicked* on Broadway before deciding to come home.

Or so he thought.

He lifted the beer and drank. What the hell was wrong with him? She was a girl he'd hung out with in high school. But he'd never even officially gone out with her, let alone slept with her.

He'd only kissed her once. And that was under duress. Why the hell was he letting her fubar his holiday—*still*—after a decade?

Christ. Wilder scrubbed a hand over his face, disgusted with himself and the whole situation.

He'd been in a damned war zone for four years and hadn't been this...whatever. Riled up. Freaked out. Unsettled.

But Tess Devine could do that to a guy, with her bossy attitude and deep chocolate eyes that just seemed to suck you down in. They could go from flashing anger to teasing to sultry in ten seconds flat. A guy didn't have a frigging chance when he took that into account along with the way she looked —all the right curves and thick honey blonde hair—plus that damned freckle on the sweet spot next to the hollow of her throat.

He might have made it home from Iraq in one piece—or mostly—but he sure as shit had a bad luck streak when it came to New Year's Eve.

Sonofabitch.

CHAPTER 3

COMING HOME WAS ALWAYS one of Tess's favorite things, but coming home at the holidays was even better. It was home, it was family, it was familiar...it was comfort.

Part of the reason was that the house, a grand Southern-style estate, was always dressed to the nines in holiday trimmings. Each year, Mom had a theme to her decor and this year, apparently, it was The Holly & The Ivy, Plus Angels. Glittering red and green holly swagged the front entrance, gold ivy curved around the banisters. Ivy topiaries trimmed with tiny red ribbons and lit by tiny white and green lights sat on the foyer table. A huge glittering tapestry of angels hung on the two-story wall above the table. And she could see a trio of elegant silver celestial beings on the fireplace mantel in the living room.

"Honey, I'm home!" Tess called gaily, dropping her Balenciaga bag on the floor and poking her head into Dad's study.

"Hi, sweet pea," he said, rising quickly from his desk chair. "*Welcome home.*" He said the words reverently, as if she'd been gone for years. So he knew. She hadn't told him much, but somehow he *knew*.

They met halfway across the room, and he looked into her eyes as if to take measure of her well-being. Then he pulled her into a tight embrace, stroking her hair like he'd done when she was little. He smelled like her daddy and she inhaled the comfort and familiarity. "Do you want to talk about it?"

Tess had managed to keep it all under control the whole day—while she was at the hospital being Belle, at Birdie's showing off fancy headpieces, talking to Deanne down-town...but now that she was home, there was no need. To her horror, she felt her eyes begin to sting and she hugged her father tighter. "Thanks, Dad," she murmured. "I needed that."

"I have a feeling you need this too, honey."

Tess turned to find her mom coming into the room, holding a big glass of red wine. She took the glass then flowed into another embrace, this time with her petite, familiar-scented mother. "Thanks, Mom," she said, taking care not to slop what was surely a zinfandel on her mother's crisp white slacks.

"You okay?" Mom asked, lifting Tess's chin even though she was five inches shorter than her daughter. Her gaze delved into hers just as Dad's had, then she nodded. "You will be." She gave her a gentle kiss on the cheek.

"I will. I'm so glad to be home for the party tonight. I thought...." Her voice wobbled, but she held it together. "I thought this would be the first year I'd miss it. Ever." *Silly. Stop being such a wuss!* Last year was the worst, when she realized she was going to have to divorce Barry.

But it had taken her almost six more months to make that decision.

"Sit, Tess. You've got about five minutes before Annabelle the whirlwind shows up—and, oh, wait till you hear about that," Mom said. Her sea-green eyes danced merrily. "She was blazing into town as usual in that little hot rod—and, well...your baby sister's streak's been broken."

"Really?" Tess asked, a smile tugging her lips. "Annabelle met her match, huh? It's about time." She sipped, then hummed with delight at the rich woodsy, berry flavor. "Ah. Thanks. I really did need that. What about Gracie—where is she? Off to Target, shopping for a dress?" Her smile turned into an affectionate laugh.

"She's upstairs trying to figure out what to wear," Dad replied with a sad shake of his head, sipping a rock glass filled with Scotch. Of the entire Devine family, including their patriarch, Grace was the only one who was clueless when it came to fashion and style. If she could, she'd wear jeans and a white t-shirt every day, just for the simplicity of it.

"She called me, wanting to know when I was going to get here so I could protect her from Belly." They all laughed together and Tess felt another pang: this one of emptiness and yet comfort, all rolled into one.

Her parents had been married for forty years, and were still as much in love as they had been when they wed. They were a united front who understood each other, adored their daughters, and yet expected the best from each of their very different offspring. They had each other.

"Tell us about it, sweet pea," Dad said, patting Tess's knee.

She drew in a deep breath and looked at them both.

"Well, it's been a little rough. The divorce. I mean, for me. Barry's been his normal self." She smiled grimly. "But I'm fine. It hasn't really hit the big press yet—only a few small outlets have picked it up. So some people know, but a lot of others don't. It probably won't go big, either, so that makes it a little easier."

No one had ever said anything overtly negative about the man she married two New Year's Eves ago during the party, but she'd sensed the distance between him and her family. And in retrospect, she understood why. They'd seen what she'd been blind to: his condescension, his attempt to control and change her, and, worst of all, his propensity for "mentoring" young actresses. On the couch.

"The divorce should be final by the end of March, but you know as far as I'm concerned, things have been over for a year. And...I left the show. I'm leaving the theater."

There. I said it.

Mom's eyes widened. She took Dad's rock glass from his hand and gulped a big swallow. When she brought the glass away she said, "You're leaving the theater?"

"Well, I'm leaving the *stage*. I'm just not...happy anymore. I know I should be grateful for the opportunity I've had, the little bit of success I've gleaned—"

"And your date with Matthew Morrison," Mom threw in. "He *was* a gentleman, wasn't he?"

Tess gave a short chuckle. "That was pretty awesome. And yes he was—unfortunately. That man is *ripped*. But there are thousands of young women who'd give anything to take my place onstage. And they probably already have," she added ruefully. "But—I'm almost twenty-nine, and thirty's just around the corner. Not old, but—I want a family. A normal life. I thought I was going to be able to do that with Barry, but...yeah. That didn't work out."

"What are you going to do?" asked Dad, just watching her.

She drew in another breath and smiled. "I'm going to do some producing, actually. Maybe being married to a director gave me the idea; I don't know. I've got some options with a couple smaller shows...in New York, but also in Chicago or Atlanta. You know I'll be good at that—bossy as I am. And that will give me more time to work with EverFun."

"You do enjoy that, don't you?" Mom said. She didn't look quite as shocked anymore. "You just light up whenever you talk about all the things you've done with that foundation —visiting the children in the hospitals, doing the fundraisers, the media interviews—everything."

"You'll be able to give your name to the Foundation, and that's good visibility for them," Dad said. "I think it's wonderful, sweet pea."

"Exactly. So—wait, is that Belly?" Tess stood, looking out Dad's study window. Sure enough, the bright red sports car was rumbling up the long drive toward the circle. She grinned, suddenly feeling lighter than she had in a long while. "Let's go hear about the cop who broke her streak!"

CHAPTER 4

NEW YEAR'S EVE: Ten Years Ago

"Mom's been bugging me to dance with Lewis Kamp-mueller," Tess hissed to Grace, peering around one of the well-lit pillars. Fortunately, the dork was nowhere in sight.

Grace laughed, tucking her light brown hair behind one ear. "Better you than me!" She smoothed her simple black dress—the one that Tess had tried to talk her out of wearing.

"You always wear black, Gracie—why don't you put on something more exciting—like red or blue or even green?" Conscious of her own emerald green gown, Tess looked around and saw her friend, David Grathwold, standing with a group of guys from school. She and David had just finished starring in their high school's production of *Annie Get Your Gun*.

"Black is simple and easy," Grace told her firmly. "I don't have time to worry about what goes with what, and whether my makeup matches, and if I have the right shoes like you do." Then she gave Tess a shrewd look. "All right, 'fess up. Are you going to kiss David at midnight or what?" Geez. She'd be a great cop.

"No, I am not going to kiss David. For Pete's sake, Grace, I kissed him enough during the show, and believe me, it didn't do a thing for me. It was like kissing a brother—if we had one. Besides, he's your age—too young for me. I'm more into college guys." Her attention wafted back to where the man in question stood with his friends. "Johnny Wilder's looking hot, though. He looks just like a young George Harrison, with those heavy brows and all that dark hair. Too bad he's too young too. And he's got a date."

"Too bad you dumped Brian last week—'cause if you hadn't, you wouldn't have to dance with Lewis," Grace pointed out.

"You're right. I should have kept him around for another week just so he could be my date. *Right*." Tess shook her head. "He was such a jerk during the show, always so jealous of David, if you can believe it. I was tired of it. And think of it this way: if I had a date, you'd be next on Mom's list—so you should be grateful for my datelessness." She smiled. "I guess I'll just have to find someone here tonight."

Grace scoffed. "Yeah, right. Like any guy you choose is going to just jump to attention when you walk by."

Tess just raised her brows and looked at her.

"Well, all right. You've got a point," her sister conceded. "They do tend to notice you. But that doesn't mean they'd *kiss* you."

"I'll bet you I can find someone to kiss at midnight. And if I do" —Tess's grin turned mischievous— "you not only have to dance with Lewis, you have to *kiss* him."

Grace paled, but considered for a moment. "All right. But, you can't count kissing Dad or any relative. And it can't just be a peck on the cheek—it's got to be on the lips. And, if you don't find someone, you have to kiss Lewis, and I'm going to tell him you have a crush on him. You only have thirty minutes, so you'd better get to work."

Tess shuddered at the idea of Lewis thinking she liked him. But the thought of her sister—tomboy Grace who only thought about studying and sports—kissing the bean pole nerd with a huge Adam's apple made her want to giggle. "Deal."

Grace insisted on bringing Annabelle into the fold as witness and the three sisters shook on it. Little did they know a New Year's Eve tradition had been born.

"Hey, guys," Tess said brightly as she wandered up to the group where David stood with his friends.

"Yo, Tess," David replied. "What's going on? Hey, do you think your dad or Mr. K will care if we get a beer from the bar?"

"If you aren't driving, I don't think one beer would be a problem. It's New Year's Eve, after all. Just don't be obvious about it—and *don't* let my Aunt Helen see you drinking it." She looked over the group of guys, searching for a potential midnight kissee.

Dang. Johnny Wilder *was* looking pretty hot tonight. She noticed his steel grey eyes and relaxed stance where he leaned against the wall. He was tall and broad-shouldered, with toned biceps that showed through the clinging shirt he wore. Didn't he know he was supposed to be wearing a suit jacket? At sixteen, he already looked more manly than the rest of them...which was probably why he had a pretty blond date who was shooting eye-daggers at Tess.

"I think we're already past one beer," Wilder drawled in his low voice. "But I wouldn't mind another one."

"All right," Tess replied, her voice automatically sliding into a matching mellow purr. Too bad he was so young. No way would senior Tess Devine lower herself to kiss a sophomore. "Anyone else want me to snag them a beer?"

In all, she promised to bring back three. She walked away from the group, trying to figure out how she was going to carry three glasses while finding someone to kiss. She'd taken a few steps toward the bar when a long steel pole shot out in front of her.

"And just what are you up to, girl?" asked a peremptory voice.

"Aunt Helen!" Tess tried to avoid the cane wielded by her great-aunt from Maine, but the old lady was too quick for her. She had to grab a table to keep from losing her balance and had barely righted herself by the time the woman placed herself in her path.

"You're going to catch your death of cold in that dress," Aunt Helen scolded, and, to Tess's acute embarrassment, reached with a claw-like hand to yank the bodice higher. "In my day and age—and it wasn't all that long ago, young lady, do you hear me?—nice young ladies wouldn't be caught dead in a dress without a bit of lace there at the throat. Here, let me see. You hold this, Teresa, now, while I find it...." She thrust her shiny cane (a new addition to her aunt's persona) at her great-niece, and upended her gauche satin pink evening bag onto a table.

Lipstick, tissues, a plastic coin case, and a little net bag filled with birdseed clunked onto an empty plate. Helen scrabbled through the debris with her curled fingers while Tess tried to think of a way to extricate herself.

"Aunt Helen, I really appreciate your help, but I need—"

"Stay right there, young lady. Don't you be walking off with that cane! I might be an old lady—not that old, mind you, but old enough to get away with whatever I wish, I'll have you know—and it's not that I need that blasted thing to get around with—'cause I don't—but it makes me look old and frail and I have found several other uses for the thing. Ah-ha!" She held up a bit of frilly lace, mussed and crumpled, and most likely smelling of moth balls.

"Aunt Helen," Tess said again, more earnestly this time. *Ten minutes to midnight.* "I need to get back to my—"

"Here we are," said her aunt. And before Tess could blink, the old lady was jamming the bit of froth right down the front of her dress.

"Aunt Helen!"

"Did you need some help, ma'am?" drawled a voice behind them.

Tess jerked away and came face to face with Johnny Wilder. Heat swarmed up from her chest, warming her face, as she met his amused gaze with her own. Great. *Caught with my great-aunt's hand down the front of my dress. Perfect.*

Helen jerked her chin up, and Tess noticed the way the termagant scoped him out. "I have everything under control, here, young man. But you can be certain that if I am in need of assistance, I'll be calling on you." Her thin lips curved in something resembling a smile.

Good grief! Was Aunt Helen flirting with Johnny Wilder?

Tess looked at the clock. *Nine minutes.* The opportunity to win her bet with Grace was slipping further away.

"You bet, Mrs. Galliday," Wilder drawled. "In the meantime, I came to see if I could help you carry those glasses, Tess. We need a fourth one."

"I would appreciate that very much." She glanced at the clock adorning the wall above the deejay, and grimaced at the time. *Eight minutes.* How was she going to swing this?

Tess slowed so Wilder walked next to her. Hm. Maybe he *could* be a candidate. She had nothing to lose (except the bet)...plus she was bold, direct, and used to getting her own way. He was only a young kid—he probably wasn't all that experienced. He'd probably jump at the chance to kiss Tess Devine.

She slanted a glance at him. If only he were a couple years older.

His arm bumped against hers, and Tess took charge. She slipped her hand around his bicep as they walked, leaning slightly into him.

Wilder glanced down at her, but he didn't draw away as they walked toward the bar. She noticed the clock hanging on the wall behind the bar. *Five minutes. Crap.* Grace and Annabelle watched from across the room. Tess looked at them and saw the matching smirks on her sisters' faces. That was it. Time was up.

"Hey Johnny," she said, gently steering him away from the bar.

He looked down again. "What's up, Tess? Aren't we going to get a beer?"

"I need a favor."

"What's that?" That drawl again—so casual and uninterested.

She pulled him toward a corner decorated by a ficus adorned with lights. They wouldn't be so noticeable here … but Grace and Annabelle could see them. Tess released his arm and looked up to catch him giving a little wave across the room. To his date. Ugh. She glanced at the big clock. *Three minutes!*

No time to lose. "See, I have a bet with my sister that I would kiss someone at midnight. So can you just kiss me real quick and then you can go back to what's-her-name?"

Surprise flared across his face and Wilder stared down at her in blatant disbelief. Tess felt her mouth dry. *Crap.* What if he refused?

"You want me to kiss you. In front of my date. In front of everyone. So you can win a bet?"

A flood of heat rushed over her face. Well, when you put it that way….But she wasn't Tess Devine for nothing. "Yes. Come on, Johnny—it's just a bet. I'll explain everything to your date. It'll be fine." She flapped her hand.

Wilder stared at her. She could read the emotions on his face: incredulity and suspicion. "And you think that'll be okay with Jilly, as long as you explain? You want to ruin the rest of my night? I have *plans*." His slow smile indicated just what he had in mind for after the party.

She rolled her eyes. "Come on, Johnny. It's just a damned kiss. For one second."

Suddenly, the atmosphere in the room shifted. The hum of voices rose, and Tess turned just as someone shouted, "It's time! Get your champagne for the midnight toast!"

She looked back at Wilder. His gray eyes were cool, and skepticism still showed on his face.

"Ten ... nine ... eight ... . " Her dad had started the countdown.

Tess glanced across the room and saw Grace grinning like an idiot. As their eyes met, Grace used her two index fingers to point excitedly toward Lewis Kampmueller, who stood only yards away. She made smooching motions with her lips and then pointed at Lewis again.

" ... Five ... four ... three ... . "

Tess swiveled back toward Wilder, who was still looking at her like she'd grown another head. She grabbed his shoulders and yanked him toward her just as the room erupted in shouts, claps, and cheers.

She missed his mouth by two inches, yet as their faces collided in the midst of the revelry, Tess felt her body shut down ... then *whoosh* alive. He turned toward her and their lips clashed awkwardly ... and then suddenly Johnny Wilder was kissing her ... really kissing her.

CHAPTER 5

PRESENT DAY

Every time Wilder walked into the Club, he couldn't help but remember the first Devine-Kampmueller New Year's Eve party he'd attended—ten years ago. That was the night Tess kissed him in order to win some sort of bet. Little did he know that was the beginning of The Curse of Tess Devine.

All his plans for Jilly Henson in the rear seat of his roomy F-10 (or on the couch in her parents' basement, or even in the hot tub room at the Club—he wasn't particular) had gone to hell the minute Tess leaned into him. Not only had that kiss left him feeling as if he'd been punched in the gut, but despite his subsequent explanations, Jilly had eventually left the party with Vance Evans—and ended up showing *him* her parents' couch in the basement.

In reality, the kiss meant nothing to either Tess or Wilder —hell, he'd kissed *a lot* of girls; he wasn't shy—but it changed things anyway.

Until that night, he knew the upperclassman Tess only as David Grathwold's co-star in the school play and the daughter of one of the most prominent families in town. Plus Grace was in his class. But since he and Grat (a junior) were tight, and Tess and Grat had become close doing the show, the three of them began to hang out together during the rest of her senior year. Sometimes Tess had a boyfriend with her, other times Wilder had a date, and usually Cara was there because everyone knew she and Grat were destined to get married as soon as they graduated. (They had.)

Heck, he and Grat used to ask Tess for dating advice. He could remember sitting at a late-night coffee session at Denny's, talking through his next move or how to ask out a girl he was hot for.

In fact, Tess had bought him and Grat their first box of condoms. He and David had been arguing about who was going to walk into Clavell's and buy them.

Tess had rolled her eyes, held out her hand for their money, and walked bold as brass into Clavell's. Moments later, she'd come waltzing out with a bag much too large for a single box of condoms. But it wasn't until they'd returned to David's house that she'd dumped the contents onto the table in front of them.

She'd bought condoms all right ... ribbed ones and lamb-skin ones, gold coins, glow in the dark ones, lubricated with and without spermicide, and even a box of extra-large. "I wasn't sure what size you guys wore," she'd teased.

And she'd purchased samples of other contraceptive methods—foams and inserts and a tube of K-Y Jelly.

"I thought I was going to shit my pants when she said she told Mr. Clavell it was for us!" Grat told him after she left.

Now, ten years later as he escorted Laney into the Club's crowded ballroom, Wilder couldn't help but glance over at the corner where he and Tess had kissed—that one and only time. What would've happened if he'd given up trying to explain his actions to Jilly and instead hung out with Tess the rest of the night?

Maybe things would have been different. But probably not. It wasn't as if he and Tess hadn't had ample opportunity to hook up over the next few years.

It was just that the circumstances had never been right.

And now she was married. To a major ass.

"What can I get you to drink?" he asked Laney, admiring the deep vee of her neckline instead of scanning the room for Tess. The dress wasn't red, but he found he didn't mind at all —black lace worked just as well when it was showcasing a generous rack like hers. Christina Hendricks didn't have a thing on his date.

"Chardonnay," she told him, her fingers curled around his arm. "Oh, look. There's Tess Devine! I haven't seen her in ages. She looks amazing. And she's *famous.*"

Famous, talented, bossy—and surrounded by rich and powerful men. She could have her pick. And she'd picked Barry Markham.

"I'll go get our drinks," he said as soon as he caught a glimpse of her heading their way. As he walked off, he heard Laney greeting Tess. *Coward.*

I'm just getting us a drink, he argued with himself.

Yeah, you beat it faster than a horny teen after his first make out session. Pussy.

I'm not hiding from her.

His inner self snickered and rolled its eyes.

Thank God there were empty stools at the bar. Wilder took a seat with his back to the ballroom, which was just across the way. With luck, he could hang out here for a few minutes until the women were done talking.

"Jameson, neat," he said to the dark-haired bartender. *Harry* was on his name tag, and although it took him a surprisingly long time to find the bottle of whiskey, he finally pushed a short glass over to him. Filled to the brim.

"Nice pour," Wilder said. *Jesus. Do I look like I need it that bad?* "A chardonnay, too."

"Right," said Harry, who turned to stare at the array of wine bottles behind him. He didn't seem to know what to do next.

"No hurry. Seriously."

"So who's the hot blonde?" Harry asked, pulling a glass down and setting it on the bar.

"Tess Devine," Wilder replied into his glass. Then he looked up, realizing he'd answered wayyy too quickly. "I mean, which one? There's a lot of hot blondes here tonight."

"Right. But only one as far as you're concerned."

Wilder frowned and looked around. What the hell? How did this guy know anything? And weren't there any other customers the guy could be serving? This side of the bar was tucked away and empty. Great. He took another sip, deciding he was in a hurry for the chardonnay after all.

But then he glanced around and saw Laney and Tess deep in conversation. They seemed to be comparing shoes. Maybe not so much in a hurry then.

"So what's the deal? You're here with the stacked brunette, but you wish you were with the blonde. Story of my life," Harry sighed. He'd poured a glass of wine all right, but it was red. Wilder was about to correct him when the bartender lifted the glass and drank from it. "Mm. Very nice." He held onto it as he leaned forward companionably. "So... old flame, ex-girlfriend, or what?"

Wilder shot him an irritated look. "Isn't that the same thing?" When Harry just raised his brows, he capitulated. "None of the above. So what's the weather saying?" He gestured to the screen above the bartender's head.

"They're calling for ice and snow later tonight. Around midnight."

"In Henderson? Are they on crack?" But when he looked at the screen, he saw the weather advisories running along the bottom of the monitor.

Harry shrugged. "I've been watching the radar. It doesn't look like they're on crack. Looks like we're going to have a white New Year's Eve."

Great. Suddenly, Johnny felt more optimistic. *Excellent excuse for leaving early. Like, asap.* "How about that chardonnay?"

"Right. They're still talking you know. And another lady joined them. You probably want to sit here a little longer." Harry grinned, then, mercifully, went to serve another customer who'd slid onto a stool nearby.

Wilder swirled the whiskey around in his glass and watched it funnel down. Ten years of Tess Devine. The first year—that hot kiss—had surprised him. The second year, he'd simply hung out with her and a group of friends, and admired from afar. But it was the next year that changed everything.

CHAPTER 6

NEW YEAR'S EVE: Eight Years Ago

Wilder had his hand down Kaylie Schwartz's dress and his mouth on her neck when a bright light broke into the darkness.

"Shit," he muttered, disengaging from her hot, sweaty skin to look up from the depths of the backseat of her car. Kaylie was beneath him, still fully clothed (but he was working on changing that), and she had her hand on his ass. He was hoping she'd move it elsewhere—like, front and center—but who the hell was out there, poking around with a light? He sure hoped it wasn't a cop. Or Mr. Devine.

He and Kaylie had been parked in the Club parking lot since one-thirty. Hadn't everyone left the party by now? He hadn't really been noticing all the cars leaving, but he'd heard the voices. And it had been quiet for a long time. Of course, he'd been a little distracted....

"Hold on," he said, aware that his voice was tight and

gritty. Well, what did you expect? He'd been looking forward to getting Kaylie into the backseat for hours.

The light was coming from a car near theirs—the only other one left in the parking lot, he realized with a shock. And it was still shining because whoever it was was digging around in the trunk—whose lights were facing the car Wilder was in.

"Johnny," Kaylie said, shifting her hips suggestively against his. "I have to get home soon."

"Right," he said, and was just about to dive back in when he saw a flash of the newcomer's face. What the hell was Tess doing out here...by herself? "Uh, hold on," he said again, and eased away. "That's Tess Devine. I'd better see what's going on."

"Tess?" Kaylie whined. "Who cares?" She moved her hand around and grabbed the front of his belt, yanking him closer. "Come on, Johnny...."

But Wilder's mom had raised his ass to be a gentleman, and a gentleman—while he might try and get lucky in the back of a girl's car whenever possible—wouldn't leave a stranded woman alone in the dark.

"I'm sorry. I better check and see what's going on. She looks like she might be in trouble." Knowing he was going to regret this, he eased away from Kaylie and slipped out of the car.

Tess turned from burrowing in her trunk (it was definitely her car because of the NYU sticker) when she heard the sound of the car door slam. "Oh crap, you scared me," she said. Then frowned. "What are you still doing here? I thought you left hours ago."

Well, she didn't seem distressed. But what the hell was

she doing out here, wearing a dark suit coat over her evening gown?

"I'm er—" He shrugged and gave her a cheesy grin. "Kaylie and I were just talking."

She glanced at the Accord with its steamed-up windows and laughed. "Talking. Right. Just make sure you're not going bareback, cowboy." She turned back to her trunk, where she seemed to be replacing a variety of things she'd taken out.

"What are you doing?" he asked, walking closer.

"I was getting my boots—my snow boots because *we* actually get snow up in New York in December."

"But we don't have it here...." He looked around, spreading his hands in question. He was still wincing over the bareback comment. Damn.

She laughed again and closed the trunk. She had a pair of snow boots in her hand. "I know. There's a problem inside and I was going to see if I could help."

"What sort of problem? And why are you still here? Didn't everyone leave, like, hours ago?"

"I was helping the band break down. They're friends of mine, you know, and I got them the gig. And I...well, they let me sing a few songs so I thought I'd help them pack up."

He remembered that. She'd gone up there and belted out "Don't Know Why" almost as well as Norah Jones herself. And then she made the keyboard player accompany her on "What Are You Doing New Year's Eve" just before midnight. And then she'd kissed a preppy-looking guy who was her date for the evening. Come to think of it, where was *he*?

"And where are they now?" He gestured to the empty parking lot. "And what about the guy you were with?"

"Aaron? Oh, he has an early flight tomorrow so he left already. The band's gone, but a couple of the catering staff and the club supervisor are still here—they're parked in the back. I was just getting ready to head home when I heard them shouting. Something happened in the spa with the hot tub and now there's a huge flood in the locker rooms, and it's going into the lounges." She shrugged. "They're trying to clean it up—there's no one to call at this time of night on a holiday—and the manager left early. I figured I'd give them a hand." She rolled her eyes. "They were totally clueless until I got them organized. But I didn't want to ruin my shoes any more than they already were, hence the boots. There's about three inches of water in there and we can't just leave it."

"Right."

As he watched, she slipped out of two flimsy looking silver shoes and shoved her feet into the boots. "So, off I go," she said, starting back toward the Club. "Remember what I said—suit up, space boy."

Wilder watched her tromp across the parking lot. She looked like a vagabond with her big clunky boots, sparkling evening gown, and black suit coat. An aggravated toot-toot of the car horn snagged his attention and he turned back to see Kaylie gesturing from the window. She didn't look happy.

He never understood what propelled him to walk over to the driver's side door and wait for Kaylie to roll down the window. If he'd just climbed in the damn car, he'd have broken the Tess Devine Curse just like that.

But, no. Thanks to his mom, he wasn't the kind of guy who could just leave. Especially since...well, Tess was here. Alone. With a bunch of people she didn't know...who knew who they were? What if they were a bunch of guys who'd been drinking while they cleaned up? Not a good idea.

"Hey, Kaylie, I'm sorry...I'm *really* sorry...but I think I better stay. There's a problem inside and Tess is helping them, and I think they could use a hand."

"Seriously?" she demanded, looking up at him with big pouty lips. One of her tits was nearly hanging out of her loosened dress.

His resolve wavered, but he held firm. "And I...uh...well, I don't have any protection with me. It's probably a good thing we were interrupted, because you were getting me pretty worked up."

Lie, lie, lie. He could practically feel the condom burning through the leather of his wallet into his ass. As if he'd come to the biggest party night of the year without a plan. To cover up the falsehood, he leaned in and gave Kaylie a kiss that nearly had him climbing back in through the window...flood or no flood.

"All right. Call me tomorrow?" she said, gunning the engine.

"For sure."

When Wilder walked back into the Club, he didn't have to search for the activity. There was a splashing, wave-like sound coming from the back of the place, and he could hear Tess barking out orders.

"No, no, we have to push the water this way, toward the lower part of the floor where it can collect. Then we can suck it up with the wet-vac—did you find it, Pete? Here, use a push-broom like I told you, Suzy. Those mops don't do a damn thing. Now you all push it this way, and I'll—Wilder? What are you doing here?"

"Another set of hands," he said, looking around. It was a disaster. She was a disaster too, with her hair in a loose ponytail and the edge of her expensive gown dragging in the water even though she'd put some sort of belt on to hold it up. She'd tossed the suit coat somewhere and her shoulders and cleavage were a very pretty thing to look at. "What can I do?"

She didn't blink, but launched into another round of orders. Find some fans, get the air conditioning turned on, empty the heavy wet-vac tank....Apparently she'd been through this before, either from a hurricane or some other flooding experience.

They all worked side by side—Wilder, Tess, two college girls from the catering staff, and Pete, the Club supervisor—for hours, trying to funnel the water out.

It was Tess who suggested they open one of the bottles of leftover champagne—"After all, Daddy and Mr. K. paid for it!"—and they all had a toast. Or two. In fact, they ended up drinking three bottles of leftover champagne, which was just enough to give everyone a nice, healthy buzz. They also raided the leftover food, which had been packed up but now became fair game as they worked.

At one point, Tess started singing "Jingle Bell Rock" as she slung her push-broom, swishing water energetically across the floor in her bright red strapless gown...and the next thing he knew, everyone joined in. They went through a slew of songs, most of which he only knew because his mom played Harry Connick, Jr. and Frank Sinatra's Christmas albums every day from December 15 through January 1.

It was the most surreal New Year's Eve he'd ever experienced in his almost-eighteen years, and weirdly enough, despite the fact that he hadn't gotten laid after all, he was having a blast. Aside from that, he couldn't believe Tess was still going. It was nearly four o'clock in the morning. After burning up the dance floor with her sisters and visiting with everyone in town all night, trying to catch up on things since she'd left for college, she should be exhausted. Even the catering staff hadn't worked as hard as she did, because he knew she'd been here with her sisters doing the decorating early in the day.

"I think we can call it a night," she finally said, surveying the area. Pretty much every drop of water had been sucked up. The two catering staff were collapsed on a sofa in the lounge, having clearly been ready to quit long ago, and Pete went to put away the wet-vac. "Or day. Or year," she added, giggling a little. "After all, it's next year now, isn't it?"

Someone was punchy. Wilder grinned. She might be bossy but she was totally hot, and really cute when she was overtired. He could see exhaustion around the edges of her eyes.

"Let's go," he said. "Mind giving me a ride home? Kaylie drove, and I don't have a car." For some reason, the thought of riding home with Tess Devine made his insides flip.

"Aww, I'm sorry things didn't work out for you tonight, Wilder," she said, slipping her arm around his shoulders in a companionable hug. She was warm and soft. Her skin glowed from the hard work, and parts of her hair fell in her face and brushed against his chin. Made it look like she'd just woken up. "Maybe next time."

"Let's go," he said, suddenly very aware of her hip bumping against him and the tantalizing view down her strapless gown...and the way she smelled. Which was amazing. His mouth dried up and as he edged slightly away, he looked up. Pete, a thirty-ish guy with a neat goatee, was looking at him with a knowing expression.

He ignored the lascivious wink and led her from the Club. This was Tess, he reminded himself. His buddy. His dating consultant. Who had no interest in him other than a kiss to win a bet because she was dating handsome, rich, twenty-something college guys like Aaron. He remembered the suit coat Tess had been wearing as they walked out to the car. Aaron didn't need his coat. So he didn't mention it.

"Want me to drive?" he asked as they approached her little Volvo wagon. "You look tired. I can drop you off then bring your car back tomorrow."

"That'd be great," she said, swaying a little. "All of a sudden, I'm whipped. And man, am I going to have blisters... and be sore...tomorrow." She sighed and settled into the passenger seat.

Even though she was exhausted, as she claimed, she still told him how to drive. When to shift. How to get to her house. To watch for deer.

"Thanks, Wilder," she said when he pulled up to her parents' house. It was dark except for an exterior light and one glowing through the front door. A motion detector light came on as he stopped in the circular drive.

He turned to say goodnight, and there she was. Right there, close as hell in the front seat. Looking all mussed and glowy and sexy as hell. Her strapless dress showed off her shoulders and the curve of her neck, and even though the light was dim, he knew there was an interesting little freckle right next to that little hollow of her throat. His mouth watered. He really wanted to kiss that mark. To lick it, suck gently on it...then move to the side of her long, elegant neck.

Their eyes met and he felt his world swim...his knees weaken...and something inside him go *ka-blam*. Like his gut just dropped. His lungs felt tight.

"You didn't have to stay, and I really appreciate it. We couldn't have done it without you," she was saying. "Thank you so much, Johnny."

"Yeah," was all he could say. *Kiss her. Kiss her!*

She's got a boyfriend.

Who gives a shit? He left early. He missed out.

She's not interested in you, Wilder.

She kissed you back two years ago.

Yeah. She sure did—

Then all at once she was climbing out of the car. "Good night, Johnny. Don't forget to wear a rain coat."

Her giddy, giggly laugh was the last thing he heard as she slammed the door and tottered inside.

CHAPTER 7

Tess couldn't find Lewis. He wasn't answering her texts either. Typical man. Typical *Lewis*. He was probably sitting in a corner somewhere, inventing a new smartphone app. That was how he'd made his millions, which, if Gracie played it right, could also be *her* millions.

Although, as she'd come to learn, money did not a happy marriage make.

But Tess needed to talk to Lewis. Not because she needed a date (at this point, she realized she didn't flipping *care*— she'd be just as happy popping a bottle of champagne on her own), but because Grace had actually had not one but *two* guys show up to be her date (nothing like overcompensating!). And neither of them looked like they were going to be easily bought off like all the other flunkies over the years had been.

Had Tess ever felt guilty about being part of the game,

working with Lewis to make sure Grace was the one he got to kiss at midnight every single year? Not really. She figured if the guys Gracie brought were as easily bought off as they had been, they didn't *deserve* her smart, funny, kickass sister—and it was a good way for her to find out.

As for Lewis...since he'd been in love with Grace forever, Tess thought the poor guy deserved a shot. A real shot. But for God's sake, he'd better make it happen this year, because she was done with the whole game.

"So where's your husband, Tess?" asked Laney Boudreau. They'd been chatting for a few minutes while Laney's date went to get her a drink. "Isn't he a director? I heard he was here last year."

"He didn't come—" she started, but Laney leapt on her words before she could explain.

"Did you bring someone else then—someone famous?" Her voice dropped to a whisper and she looked around as if expecting to see George Clooney step out of the shadows.

I wish.

Tess could have been irritated by the celebrity stalking, but she wasn't. After all, one year she'd brought the lead singer of Grammy winner Ferrie's Wake, and another time she'd brought Senator Goldstein's son.

She'd gotten used to this sort of reaction from the members of her hometown, and realized they were simply curious. And a little intimidated. They read gossip magazines and Page Six and entertainment blogs and just wanted to know what it was really like to have Matthew Broderick and Sarah Jessica Parker know you by name, and run into Jon Stewart at the Rockefeller Center and actually have a conversation, and know where Beyonce and Jay-Z's apartment was because you'd been there.

So she replied with the patience and grace she'd cultivated when dealing with these situations. "I'm actually here without a date tonight. It's a little strange, but I'm getting divorced, and, well, I just wanted to have a relaxed time tonight. Especially since it's technically my second anniversary. But," she added with a purposeful twinkle in her eye (she wasn't an actress for nothing), "if you see any hot, single guys, send 'em my way."

"Oh, I'm really sorry you're getting divorced," Laney replied. She seemed sincere. "I hadn't heard anything—I mean, in the gossip columns. Well," she looked a little mortified at having to admit it, "I do read Page Six. It's kind of neat when someone you sort of know shows up in it."

"I read Page Six too," Tess confessed with a smile, casting a subtle glance around for Lewis. Where was he? It was after ten. "And the divorce hasn't really made the news—we're definitely not a big celeb couple like Brangelina or whatever they're calling Ryan Reynolds and Blake Lively. Which is fine with me."

"So does that mean *you'll* have to kiss Lewis Kampmueller tonight instead of Grace?" Laney said with a broad smile.

Tess chuckled. Pretty much everyone knew about the arrangement (after all, it had been going on for a decade), and most people knew about the behind-the-scenes manipulation Lewis always did to make sure he kissed the right Devine girl. Except for Grace. "Well, it's definitely looking that way. I hope Gracie doesn't get jealous."

They were laughing together when Tess noticed her

mother gesturing to her from across the room. "Excuse me, Laney," she said, turning back to her companion. "Looks like my mother needs to talk to me—probably about whether the band's been paid yet. You have a great time the rest of the night!"

It took her longer than it should have to make her way across the room—but it was to be expected. Everyone wanted to know how she was doing, where her date was (apparently news of her divorce was just beginning to filter around), when her next Broadway appearance was going to be (she didn't say), and whether she was actually going to have to kiss Lewis this year.

She finally extricated herself from Mr. and Mrs. Turniter and, ready to make a beeline toward Belly, turned abruptly. And came face to face with Johnny Wilder.

"Oh," she said in an embarrassingly gaspy sort of way. "Wilder." *Crap.* That still came out sounding like Marilyn Monroe. "Hi. I didn't know you were in town." *Oh my God, could you sound more idiotic?*

"Same here," he drawled. He had that way of speaking so low and carelessly...it felt like a little caress down her spine. "Didn't expect to see you."

Well, that's about as blunt as you can get, isn't it? "Last minute change of plans," she said, trying to smile casually.

Tess could not figure out why her heart was literally slamming in her chest. Johnny Wilder was just an old friend...well, yeah, who'd said some things during an opportunistic moment—but, Lord, one look at him and he was pushing *all* her buttons tonight. He was like a tall, cool drink on a summer day: mouthwatering.

His hair needed a cut, but it looked good—a rich bronzy

brown brushing the collar of his tux and in thick waves curling back from his temples. The last time she'd seen him, it was cut military short for the Air Force. His mouth was fixed in a familiar half-smirk but his eyes wouldn't quite meet hers. Tess had seen hundreds of sexy men in tuxes, but there was something about the way he wore his—with careless attitude —that really made her hormones buzz. He looked so cool and sharp: the crisp white shirt under the sleek black coat encasing broad shoulders, military straight and a stance filled with confidence. He wore a neat, understated black bow tie and sharp onyx cufflinks. It was a delicious package and her insides were all a-flutter.

"So...it's been a while," she said after an awkward moment. "A few years. I heard you were in Iraq. I'm glad you made it back safely...." Her voice trailed off. Surely war had changed him. Maybe that was why he carried himself so differently...with an attitude, and strength, and something else. A subtle show of...not bravado but...wisdom? Experience. And not the kind with women, though he had that in spades too. "I'm sure you look at things differently now."

His eyes widened a little as if he wasn't expecting such a personal and intuitive comment and he seemed to relax slightly. "I do. It was...dark. And difficult. But there were moments of satisfaction and victory. I was proud to be there. Glad I went."

"Thank you," she replied. Meaning it.

Then, "Hey," she said, trying to jolt herself out of this very strange discomfort. She tested a little flirtatious smile. "I don't have a date tonight, and since I'm really not interested in kissing Lewis Kampmueller, maybe you could help me out again? You know, for old times' sake?" She forced herself to sound light and funny and teasing, just the way she'd always been with Wilder. Pretending she didn't remember anything that had happened four years ago.

His gray eyes swept over her, suddenly turning Arctic cold. "I don't think your asshat of a husband would appreciate that. Nor would my very sexy date. Good to see you again, Tess." And he walked away.

Her cheeks flared hot and her whole body quivered with anger even as it flushed with shame.

Four years ago, he'd been playing the "I'm off to war, honey, send me off with a bang," card….

Damn good thing she hadn't believed him.

CHAPTER 8

NEW YEAR'S EVE: Four years ago

"This was a great idea, Tess," said Grat. "I've been wanting to see *Iron Man*, but with two kids it's a little hard to get out of the house."

"My pleasure," she replied, gesturing them into the home theater in her parents' basement. "Get comfortable. We've got all the leftover beer and wine—no champagne though—and some food. Wilder, you open a few bottles. Cara, can you get the plates? They're in the cupboard over there. And napkins too. Grat, some of us—like me—will want blankets. They're in the trunk by the wall. Gracie, here's the DVD. Brooks, can you light the fire? It's real wood, so you might have to use your Boy Scout skills instead of flipping a switch."

The annual Devine-Kampmueller bash had ended unusually early due to a widespread case of the flu throughout Henderson. The few people who'd actually made it to the party had cleared out shortly after midnight, either because their children were home sick, they were getting sick or had just gotten over being sick, or because it simply wound down early. Even Belly wasn't feeling well and had slipped off to bed right away.

So Tess had invited a group of friends over to watch *Iron Man* and whatever other movies they could get to.

"Too bad Barry had to miss the party," Grace said when she handed her the DVD. "But at least you got to show off your new rock tonight."

Tess lifted her hand, loving the way the low lights in the room caught at the sparkles of the three-carat diamond. "Poor guy. He was so sick he couldn't even make his flight. If I'd known, I would have just stayed instead of flying down here so early. Go put that disk in, and let's get started. You know how much I love Robert Downey, Jr."

They drank beer and wine and watched *Iron Man*, then someone put in *Love, Actually* (over which the guys groaned and the gals sighed) and by then, it was past four. And everyone had had more than enough to drink.

"We'd better hit the road," Grat said, helping Cara to her feet. "Even though our babysitter is staying the night, I'm done. I haven't been up this late since college. You okay to drive, honey, because I'm sure not."

Grace yawned. "I'm off to bed too. I'll help clean up in the morning, Tess."

"See you all tomorrow. You'll be over to watch the game, right?" said Brooks.

"You mean later today," Tess replied, realizing the room was wavering a little. "Yes, we wouldn't miss game day at the Bennetts'!" *Whew. That last glass of wine really did me in.* But the warmth of a perfect buzz filtered through her and she was still wide awake—thanks to her nocturnal schedule back home.

Grace tromped up the stairs to say goodbye to Brooks and the Grathwolds, and Tess turned to put a few things away.

"Hey Wilder. Don't tell me you want me to put in another chick flick. I've got a bunch of them," she teased. "We could do *The Sound of Music* or *Pride & Prejudice*. Or how about *The Ugly Truth*. That'd be perfect for you."

"No thanks." He was gathering up plates and cups and setting them on the counter. "But I don't think I'd better drive tonight. Can I crash here?"

"Definitely." Tess wandered over and poured herself another glass of wine. "I'm not ready to go to bed yet myself, but I'm not interested in another movie. Want something?"

There was a pregnant pause that had her glancing up at him when he didn't immediately reply, then he said, "A beer. Thanks."

By the time she got the beer opened, he'd settled on the floor in front of the fire, leaning back against a heavy coffee table, his feet flat on the ground. The plush cream-colored rug was inviting, and Tess sank down next to him as she handed over the beer.

"I miss having a real fire," he commented. "Mom's got a gas fireplace, but there's nothing like the smell of real wood burning."

"Feels a little weird to have one when it's so warm out, but a fire says the holidays to me," Tess replied. "And it's a little chilly down here."

She stretched out her legs with a soft groan, pointing her bare feet toward the fire. Because it was her house, she'd had the luxury of changing into yoga pants and a t-shirt, but

Wilder was still in his tux. He'd taken off his coat and tie and rolled up his sleeves. The top two buttons of his shirt were undone too, showing a hint of the silver chain from his dog tags in a teasing vee of dark hair.

Tess looked away from that tantalizing sight and sipped her wine. "So basic training is done and now you're being sent to Arizona. Any chance you might end up...overseas?"

"A very good chance," he replied in that rumbly drawl. It always snaked up her spine like a delicious little stroke. "Because I've been in the National Guard since high school, I'm more likely to be deployed to a...less friendly place."

"Be safe, Johnny Wilder," she said, nudging him companionably with her elbow. She felt mellow, warm, soft...and the room was like a nice little cocoon, pressing down on her.

"I intend to." He rose and she watched him walk a little unsteadily across the room.

His hair was short, buzzed in military style, and he held himself differently too. The severe cut made him look so very serious and mature, especially with his dark brows and very square jaw. Tess drew in a shaky breath. She'd stopped thinking of Johnny Wilder as a too-young boy years ago.

Her insides fluttered a little when she remembered the one kiss they'd shared, and the subsequent years of subtle awareness between them. Or at least, the subtle awareness she had for him. Definite animal attraction on her part. But she knew better than to let herself get interested in Wilder. He got around quite a bit (which was why she always ragged on him about wearing a condom), and she had a good idea how his mind worked when it came to women. After all, they'd been discussing his so-called love life for years. The nicest term for him when it came to women was "opportunist."

And there'd been the New Year's Eve two years back when they'd both been at the annual shindig with different people. She and Wilder had somehow ended up texting each other harmless, naughty little notes from across the room. She didn't even remember how it started....

Oh, right. It was after she got up and sang "Santa Baby" with the band, vamping it up with her very best Marilyn Monroe/Madonna impression. She was in a sassy, fuchsia gown and Tess knew she had the attention of pretty much every guy in the room—except for Wilder. He had an arm slung around his date's shoulders, whispering in her ear, making her giggle. Even from the stage, she could see his fingers playing with the ends of her hair and it was kind of sexy. Okay, really sexy.

Which was why, when she returned to Bill, her date, she was surprised to find a text message on her phone. From Wilder.

Thought Billy-Bob was gonna have a heart attack when u looked @ him like that. During song. Guy's whipped.

I do my best, she wrote back, grinning at her phone. *Maybe u and Betsy should get a room.*

Been there, done that.

Hope u weren't bareback, cowboy. Gotta take care of urself. Don't be stupid. World isn't ready for ur offspring!

Never stupid. U and Billy-Joe look bored. U should get a room.

Ha. Third date. U know I don't do it on the third date.

No wonder he looks like that. Guy's messed up.

Then, a while later after she'd danced crazily with her

sisters, sang another song ("I'll Be Home for Christmas") and had more champagne, she received this message:

Why don't you blow off Jim-Bob and come with me to get some more beer...or something.

What about Betsy?

What about Betsy? he replied. *Non-issue. Let's blow this place. U and me.*

Ha! You'd be so lucky!!

Just think of what we could do with ur body. And my tongue.

Even now, Tess remembered the shock of heat and vivid imagery that rushed through her when she saw that response. *Whoa.* How much had he had to drink? She wasn't sure how to respond, so she sent back a quick *LOL* after a few minutes. She didn't see Wilder after that—come to think of it, she wasn't even sure he was still at the party when he sent that last message.

But the following year—which was last year—she remembered that provocative message. Well, to be honest, she'd thought about it many times over the year. Maybe she should pursue it. She'd always found him sexy as hell. So she texted him the day after Christmas and said, *What're u doing New Year's Eve? ;-) Want to go to party w me?*

His response...the next day...was: *Sorry. Got plans.*

So that was that. A whole year of wondering, hoping, waiting...fantasizing. And he didn't come to the big party that night either. So apparently, it really had just been talk.

Now, sitting in her parents' basement in front of the fire, Tess knew any chance she might have had to test out her attraction to Johnny Wilder was gone. She was engaged to be married, and his flirtations had always been just that: spur of the moment titillation. Beer (or wine) goggles.

Which was why when he turned off the lights, her pulse didn't even spike. She agreed with his implicit opinion: it was too late for bright lights, and the fire was beautiful.

Wilder settled back on the floor next to her. "Much better," he murmured. The firelight played over his face and warmed her toes and Tess felt soft and mellow.

"So you're doing really well on Broadway," he said, glancing at her. "That's amazing, Tess. But not really. You've always had it all: looks, talent, drive. I admire that—that you went after what you wanted."

"Thanks," she said, staring into her glass. "It's pretty wonderful. I get to do something I love to do for a living. There aren't many people who do."

"No."

"But there are times when...well, it feels...oh, I don't know...." Tess sipped, tasting the full-bodied wine thoughtfully. "I don't know." She glanced at him and saw his profile, for he stared straight into the dancing flames. A strong nose and square jaw and full, sensual lips. A small wave of regret washed over her. *I'll never kiss him again. I'll never find out... what if?* Her heart was racing.

"It feels...what?" he asked, low and gritty, still staring at the fire.

"It's going to sound silly. Or...too esoteric or pompous or something." She gave a little chuckle and bumped his foot with hers. "I've had too much wine and I'm not making any sense." She slumped down lower against the coffee table. Maybe she'd just go to sleep right here.

"You can tell me. I'd like to know what's going on in your mind, Tess Devine."

She laughed again and elbowed him this time. "Don't tease me. But, fine. Since you insist. I haven't told anyone else this because...it'll sound—oh, I don't know—ungrateful is the word."

"Can you get to the point?" Gentle exasperation filled his voice. "Just say it."

"Well, being onstage is wonderful. A dream come true. But theater is so...superficial. And fake. Everyone's always playacting—onstage and elsewhere. And it's...cutthroat. Sometimes. At least, it feels to me. Like there's no real *purpose* for it. No benefit to mankind, no altruistic aspect. Not like—you know—joining the service. Serving your country. All I do is stand up there and help people waste a couple hours of their time."

Tess looked at him, realizing sharply that he could leave... be shipped out...and she might never see him again. He could be sent off to the Middle East, and the worst could happen.

"Nothing wrong with a little entertainment," he murmured. "Everyone needs a laugh, or a way to get their mind off maybe something bad happening in their lives. You give people an escape. That's important too."

"I told you it would sound stupid," she sighed. "And ungrateful."

"So you're getting married," he said after a short silence. His voice was so low she could hardly hear it over the snapping of the fire.

"Yes. A year from now. Maybe two, depending how quickly we can get things together. We thought it would be neat to get married on New Year's Eve. Oh, but you've met him. I forgot. At your sister's wedding last summer."

"Yep. I met him. Barry." There was a tone to his voice. "I don't think you should marry him, Tess."

"Why not? You think I'm too young?" Her short chuckle was sort of choked off because of the way she was slumped down. "I'm twenty-six. Great age to get married."

"Yeah. That's it. You're too young." He gave a short, gritty laugh and drank from his beer.

"I'm in love with you."

Tess blinked. Her whole body went still...inside and out. She dared not breathe. Had she just heard what she thought she heard? Or was it the wine and the lateness of the night and the fact that his voice was so low she could hardly discern what he was saying? She really didn't know. Her mind was swimming, her body was alive and filled with odd, rocketing sensations and she tried, *tried*, to re-imagine the moment...the words he'd muttered.

"What did you say?" she breathed after a moment.

"Hm?" He was staring into the fire.

Her heart was pounding. *Stop it. You didn't hear him right. Wishful thinking, maybe? No, Tess, every man doesn't have to fall for you. Even one you've wanted for a long time.*

And you're engaged to Barry, whom you love. Don't be stupid.

"I...nothing." She finished the last of her wine. It was time for bed. She was hearing things—things she didn't want to hear.

"Do you have any idea how intimidating you are?"

"Wh-what?" Again she rolled her head along the edge of the coffee table to look at him. She was so confused.

"Makes it hard for a guy to...." His laugh was short and self-deprecating. "I've been trying to catch you between boyfriends for years. Every single New Year's Eve. And now you're getting married. We could have had a really good time, Tess. You and me. It would have been...*amazing*."

Suddenly she was rigid all over. Very nearly holding her breath. Because she knew if he touched her...reached for her —maybe even looked at her—she'd be done. That'd be it. She'd be breaking her vows before she even took them. Yet she fairly quivered with anticipation and attraction.

Johnny, why didn't you tell me this before? she wanted to say. *Why did you wait till I found someone? It's too late.*

She couldn't think of any response that wouldn't sound desperate or suggestive or sharp. He was drunk. She was well past tipsy. The chemistry between them blazed.

Anything she said could lead to something she'd regret in the morning.

They sat in silence for a long time, staring at the fire. And sometime later, she fell asleep.

CHAPTER 9

Well, that went well. Better than he'd expected.

Wilder walked away from Tess with easy strides, feeling, for the first time fully confident of himself around her. He was no longer the fumbling, intimidated young man who adored the bright and shining, unattainable star.

Christ—he snorted at himself—*did I actually think those words? Bright and shining star? Unattainable?*

"Oh there you are, John. I've been looking all over for you." His mother's voice penetrated his thoughts and pulled him right out of the depths.

"Hi Mom. Hey Rick," he added, glancing at his mother's date, then back at her. "You look great," he remembered to say, then realized it was true. His mom looked hot. Really hot. He caught Rick's eye and gave him a cool warning look. *Spanks. Christ.* Now he felt vaguely ill.

Rick grinned and affectionately jostled his date. "Your son's giving me the hairy eyeball."

"He does that sometimes," she replied, looking totally pleased with herself. "But now he's going to dance with his mother, because it's after ten already."

Wilder didn't see how he had any choice, so he handed Laney's chardonnay to Rick and asked him to deliver it to her. Then he set his own drink down and led his mother out to the dance floor. Thank God it wasn't a fast dance; he just couldn't imagine swiveling hips in front of his mom, or, worse, watching *her* swivel hips in front of him.

"What's wrong?" she asked as soon as they embraced then moved into an easy swaying motion, his hand on her waist, hers on his shoulder.

"Nothing's wrong," he said. Then he realized that only three couples away, Tess was dancing with Brooks Bennett. Which put her directly in his line of sight. She was facing toward him at the moment, giving him an unwanted view of herself.

Usually she wore her hair down, long and full and morning-after sexy. But tonight, someone had spent a lot of time doing it up in a loose, messy style. He'd been close enough to see a myriad of tiny braids and curls and sparkling clips, all pulled together in a disordered mess of honey-bronze-platinum. Her dress tonight was the color of a rich, full-bodied red wine with a high, modest neckline that cut away to bare her shoulders like an athletic swimsuit—and, thank God, hid that sexy freckle by her throat. Her only jewelry was a wide glittering bracelet. Probably real diamonds from her dickwad husband.

"Don't lie to your mother," said his mother. "I can tell

when something's wrong. You were talking to Tess Devine...." Her voice trailed off knowingly. "Tell me what's wrong."

"Mom, there's nothing to tell." He'd shifted them around so he didn't have to look at Tess, and he actually believed those words. Over and done with. Time to move on from the Curse of Tess Devine.

"She's getting divorced, you know," his mother announced. "I just heard."

He very nearly stopped in his tracks, but suddenly aware of how closely she was scrutinizing him, he managed to hide his shock. "Oh?" *Oh shit.* Wilder suddenly felt as if the floor was falling away beneath his feet. What had he said...something about her *asshat husband?* Who was an asshat, no doubt, but still....

Maybe he wasn't as good at hiding his reaction as he thought—or maybe it was just because it was his mother, but she squeezed his shoulder. "You've had a thing for her for a long time, haven't you?"

No. Yes. How the hell did you know? "What?" seemed like the safest response.

"Well, at least you aren't denying it," she said, looking up at him shrewdly. "Maybe we're making progress."

"What are you talking about?" They'd shifted around again, and he was once more facing his New Year's Eve Curse...but this time he had a view of her long, elegant, *naked* back. On which Brooks had settled one large hand...right above her ass.

Whoa. Suddenly he could hardly swallow. It looked so damn modest from the front...until you saw it from the rear. He swore he could make out the beginning of her bottom... those two sweet indentations right above the nice sassy curve.

And her hair was up, so he could see where the wide halter buttoned with three glittering garnet fasteners at the nape of her neck.

He peeled his eyes away and realized he hadn't given a damned thought to Laney since he caught a glimpse of Tess. *Frigging idiot, Wilder. How many more New Year's Eves are you going to let her fubar?*

"Oh, look—there's Harry Devine. I've been wanting to dance with him. Hi Harry," said his mom in a very loud voice as the song came to an end...and because the band was killer, they knew better than to give their audience a chance to slip from the dance floor, so they went right from "Unforgettable" into "Lady in Red" with hardly a change of chord.

"Do you mind if I claim this next dance with your father, Tess? You can dance with him any time," Mom was saying as she intercepted Mr. Devine, who was just relieving Brooks from his dance with Tess.

The next thing Wilder knew, he was facing Tess in the middle of the dance floor. *Right* in the middle, so there was no easy escape. Her face was stony, which, could he blame her?

"Guess we're dancing," he said, trying out his signature grin, and reached for her. "And, hey, it's your song—'Lady in Red.'" He gestured to her sparkling cabernet gown.

"I wouldn't want to upset your *very sexy* date," she hissed. But her cheeks had high patches of red on them that he was pretty sure wasn't makeup.

"I'm sorry," he said. "My comment was uncalled-for."

"It certainly was," she snapped. They weren't dancing, but more like facing off in the middle of a crowd of people. Strobe lights flickered around and over them and the music was loud enough that he could hardly hear her, let alone anyone else. "My ex-husband might be an asshat, but that's beside the point. I hope you have better luck getting into your *very sexy* date's pants than you did to mine. She might fall for your lines, but I sure didn't."

With that, she turned and flounced away.

CHAPTER 10

AFTER THEIR LITTLE tete-a-tete on the dance floor, Tess hadn't seen Wilder again for well over an hour...which was just fine with her. He was probably shoving his hand down his *sexy date's* dress in some dark corner. That made her doubly glad she'd never fallen for his moves.

And....She sighed. It was almost midnight, and she hadn't found Lewis anywhere. Texts to him had gone unanswered. She guessed it would be pretty darn hard to kiss the guy if he wasn't even present, so she figured the bet was off...even though she'd pretty much decided she was going to kiss him this year. Why not?

Annabelle seemed to be missing, and Grace was in what looked like some heavy conversation with her two dates. Or maybe they weren't dates at all. For all she knew, Grace could be in the middle of some FBI stakeout and the two hotties were her team.

So neither of her sisters would notice if she kissed Lewis or not. She was off the hook. They were all off the hook.

"Where are you going, young lady?" From nowhere, a clawlike hand grabbed Tess's arm. "It's nearly midnight."

"Aunt Helen." Tess tried to keep her lack of enthusiasm from being too obvious. "I was just...going to check the coat room over here to see—"

"Don't you have a handsome young man to kiss? What about the one you were just dancing with? *He* looks like he'd be able to take out that pansy you married, and with one blasted hand behind his back." She spoke with relish, her silvery beaded handbag dancing violently from the handle of her cane.

"Vance? Oh, he's not exactly my type. Besides, I think he and Brooks and the other cops are going to get called into work. That supposed ice storm is really happening," Tess replied, and at that moment noticed a glint on the floor near the coat room. She bent and picked up a breathtakingly lovely evening shoe. It looked almost like a glass slipper—but it was even more gorgeous than any Cinderella had ever worn. "A Louboutin," she breathed. "What on earth is this doing here? And where's the other one?"

"What's that?" Aunt Helen screeched. "A lobo-what?" She stamped her cane on the ground. "Don't know how anyone could walk in those durned things. Heel must be six inches tall!"

"Oh, but it's worth it," Tess said, slipping her foot in just to try it out. Gorgeous. And expensive. Whoever lost it would definitely be wanting it back.

But she didn't want to leave it where it might be seen—or stolen. So she slipped it behind the coat room entrance, tucking it around the corner on the floor, and turned to attend to her great-aunt who was still babbling on about something.

"What about that Wilder boy?" Aunt Helen was demanding. At the top of her lungs. Thank goodness they weren't in the ballroom, but instead were at the coat room. "You've always had a thing for him since you were serving him beer when you all were too durned young to be drinking it!"

"What?" Tess couldn't believe the old bat could remember that far back, and in such detail.

"Oh, don't think I didn't notice that, Tessy girl. I've helped solve murders, you know. I see things even Adrian Monk wouldn't notice." Aunt Helen stomped with her cane again, and her evening bag slid to the floor.

Like the well-trained niece she was, Tess stooped to pick it up and noticed it bore a marked resemblance to her own handbag...which reminded her she'd left it on the table behind the band. "We've been friends for a long time," she said. "But it's never been anything more than that."

"Hmph." Aunt Helen clearly did not believe her, even though Tess was speaking the truth. "Seems to me, missy, you'd be better off with a man who's been in love with you for ten years than that philandering sneak you married."

Tess gaped at her. She wasn't certain which part of her comment she found more objectionable—and she certainly didn't have any idea how to respond that wouldn't get her in trouble with Mom. Just went to show that even eagle-eyed Aunt Helen was wrong sometimes.

"I'm not gonna tell you I had a chance to be married, Teresa—b'cause I didn't. I never found a man could keep up with me, or one I respected enough. Back in my day, we was told to be quiet and let the *man* make the durned decisions. Take the lead. Have the career. Pah! I wasn't ever going to let *that* happen. But a pretty girl like you shouldn't have the same trouble I did—men're different now." She wagged a crooked finger in her face, her dark eyes gleaming furiously.

"Right," Tess said, nodding, trying to keep her expression bland. *Back away slowly.* "It's almost midnight, Aunt Helen. And it looks like something's going on in there—look, Grace is up onstage. With Dad." *Oh boy.*

Tess's heart squeezed. Even with *two* dates her sister couldn't make it happen? *Poor Grace.*

"What? Where's her date? Didn't she have *two* men here with her? Can't you durned Devine girls do *anything* right?" Aunt Helen stomped off as fast as she could go with her handbag thumping against her cane.

Tess heaved a sigh of relief and turned...just in time to see Lewis Kampmueller rush through the door of the Club. He looked wild and a little mussed.

"You're...here," she said, looking at him curiously. He looked...different.

"Yeah." He seemed to be slightly addled—but that wasn't unusual for Lewis. If he wasn't coding an app in his head, he was trying to remember something he wasn't supposed to have forgotten. "Uh...."

"Just in time for midnight. I should have known you wouldn't miss it," she said grimly. She glanced around the corner and saw Grace, still onstage next to Dad. Alone.

And she looked at Lewis. "It's less than two minutes till midnight. I think you should kiss me tonight."

He looked at her, looked around, and glanced toward the ballroom, where everyone was gathered. It was noisy—boos, shouts, catcalls, and the sound of clinking glasses as the waiters distributed champagne flutes. "Uh...."

"One minute!" someone called from the next room.

"I—" Lewis began, and Tess took matters into her own hands.

This is for Grace. She stepped toward him, grabbing his upper arms—noticing they were surprisingly firm and muscular—and said, "Let's just kiss each other and be done—"

"Why break your streak now, Tess?" A drawling voice from behind had her whirling from Lewis. "After all, it's been ten years. You've never lost the bet yet."

From the next room: *Ten!*

"Oh, hi Johnny," Lewis said as casually as if they'd just run into him at the store.

Nine!

But Wilder was looking at Tess. His eyes were iron gray. Determined and cool. But his voice was still low and even. "It's time to end this curse. And the best way to end it is...the way it began."

Eight!

"Nicely," Wilder said, advancing toward her, "and neatly."

Her heart was thumping wildly and she was hardly aware when Lewis ducked away, out of sight. The only thing she was aware of was Wilder. Tall, dark, broad-shouldered, and very cool. In control. Her knees wobbled.

Seven!

"But what about your sexy d—"

The rest of her words were cut off as he curled his hand behind her head and pulled her to him, almost lazily...almost as if he knew she wouldn't resist. Then he covered her lips hungrily, just roughly enough to let her know he was in charge.

The kiss—deep and long and slick—was enough to make her toes curl, her knees buckle, her world contract into that moment of hot, sensual onslaught. Because it wasn't gentle or tender...it was an arrogant kiss, a demanding one. A thorough one.

She opened her eyes when he pulled away and Tess realized she'd grasped Wilder by the front of his shirt and was holding on for dear life. She was breathing heavily and her lips throbbed. Her whole body was hot and shivery and alive.

"Wow," she breathed—and was amazed she even managed that.

"For the last time: Happy New Year, Tess." He brushed her cheek with a gentle finger, then turned and walked away...just as the next room erupted with the sound of "Auld Lang Syne."

"Happy New Year!"

She stared after him. *Holy crap.* What have I done?

CHAPTER 11

ONE O'CLOCK IN THE MORNING.

"You're kidding me, right, Mom? I just navigated home in the worst ice storm Henderson's ever had and you want me to go *back* there?" Wilder was incredulous. "For a damned mink stole? What happened to worrying about me all the time? Wouldn't it worry you to send me back out in this mess?"

"You were in the Air Force in Iraq for three years," she replied mildly. "And as you've reminded me countless times, you can pilot fighter jets and navigate space shuttles. I think you can manage to drive four miles in an ice storm in an SUV."

Wilder just gaped at her. She was dressed in a fluffy pink bathrobe, holding a glass of wine. And Rick was standing behind her, in sweats and a sweatshirt. He looked very comfortable—as opposed to Wilder, who was still in his tux, sans his very sexy date, and once again alone on New Year's Eve. And he'd just driven home on a sheet of ice.

"It's a mink stole, Mom. How could you forget a *mink stole?* It'll still be there tomorrow. I'll go back first thing in the morning."

But she gave him a mutinous look. "Someone might take it. Do you know how much those things cost? And Rick gave it to me for Christmas...I've only had it for a week! I forgot it because they were rushing us out the door because the roads were getting bad."

He still couldn't believe her insistence. Why the hell didn't she send *Rick* to get it? Then he looked at the older man and realized exactly why she wanted him out of the house. And all of a sudden, he was fine with *not* being in the same building while his mom and her boyfriend were...doing whatever. *Spanks.* He shuddered. "Fine. I'll go. But if I end up in the ditch, *you're* coming to dig me out," he told her. "And don't expect me back soon. It'll take at least fifteen minutes to get there. *If* I don't go off the damned road."

He slammed out the door, leaving Rick and his mother watching in his wake.

"What if there's no one there to let him in?" Rick asked, rubbing a hand down her spine. He had that look in his eyes, and Sandra Wilder knew what that meant.

"Oh, there's someone there," she replied, smiling up at him.

He lifted an eyebrow. "Apparently there's something you're not telling me. Well, at any rate, we might want to get busy...before he returns."

She shook her head and linked her arm through his. "We have all the time in the world. He won't be back tonight."

❋

The only good thing about being sent back out in the sleek, slippery, dark night was that Wilder had something on which to focus his mind.

Unfortunately, aside from the hair-raising drive, his thoughts weren't terribly pleasant.

First was the fact that Laney had seen him kissing Tess, which just went to prove that Tess Devine really was his New Year's Eve curse. The gift that just kept on giving. He didn't even try to explain to his date—it was moot. She had a right to be furious, and she didn't give a damn about any bet or curse or anything else.

He knew this because he got an earful *all* the way back to her house. Which took a lot longer than usual because of the weather...which made for an even more unpleasant, tense trip.

He wasn't thinking about kissing Tess, though the hot memory fought him at the edges of his mind. That was one thing he needed to keep out of his thoughts. But that didn't mean he wasn't remembering every other damn New Year's Eve she'd ruined.

Like last year. She'd emailed him, wishing him a Happy New Year. A chatty message, a hey-how're-ya-doing message. Would love to see you kind of thing. He was in Florida, at a party with a date he was sort of into, fully aware Tess was married—and it still screwed his evening because he couldn't help but *wonder*...and that fubarred his night.

When Wilder pulled into the parking lot at the Club, he wasn't surprised to find it empty. He figured that would be the case, but—wait. There was one car. And a dim light from the depths of the building.

Well, maybe he'd get the mink stole after all. At least he'd have something to keep him warm if he ended up in the ditch on the way home—a definite possibility, based on the number of 360s he'd done on the way here.

He trudged through the sleet and ice, nearly falling on his ass because he was still wearing his damned dress shoes. When he passed by the car and noticed the New York license plates, he nearly fell again because he stopped so fast.

Really? What were the chances?

Actually, pretty damn high. And not just because of the curse thing. Tess always stayed late because she arranged for the entertainment, and hung around to pay them and make sure they got packed up. But what the hell was she still doing here?

Unless...maybe she went home with someone else and left her car here. That was probably the case. But he better check anyway.

He relaxed a little and went on toward the Club, expecting to find the door locked and nobody home. Wrong. The door was unlocked and, heart beating, palms ridiculously damp, he let himself in.

Everything was silent and dark except for the faint light spilling from the back of the Club and a quiet rumbling sound. Remnants from the party littered the place because, apparently, even the staff had left early. An ice storm in Henderson was nothing to sneeze at—even though his mother thought it was a walk in the park.

Confetti, champagne flutes (empty and half-filled), chairs in disarray, hats and horns and balloons...geesh. The crew was going to have their work cut out for them when they returned tomorrow. Although it looked as if most of the food was put away. And the band, he noticed, had packed up, for the stage was empty.

Following the glow of light and the rumbling noise, Wilder headed toward the back, where the spa and lounges were...and then he recognized the sound. A bubbling hot tub.

He stopped, wary. But he had to know for certain. Years ago, there'd been that flood. Who knew if the ice storm tonight had caused the pipes to burst and there was another mess that Tess was trying to clean up. On her own.

"Hello?" he called, figuring it was best to announce himself...just in case. "Anyone here?"

He heard a splash as he approached the entrance to the spa area and hesitated. "Hello?" He peered around the corner and froze at the sight that greeted him. *Well.* That was a titillating image if he'd ever seen one.

"Wilder! What are you doing here?" Tess lowered the *gun* she'd been pointing in his direction, and set it on the edge of the hot tub next to her.

But, honestly, he hardly noticed the weapon. Instead, he was looking at her...at his accursed Tess: all flushed and glowing and damp from the hot tub bubbling and foaming around her. The fact that her shoulders were bare and her red gown was slung over a chair told him his teen-aged fantasies had come true...sort of. (A gun had never figured into them when he was seventeen.)

Her hair was still up, all different shades of golden curls and braids, just beginning to sag. He could see that fascinating freckle right next to the hollow of her throat and thought it was one of the most provocative things he'd ever seen. She wore something red and glittery at her ears, and the wide diamond cuff around her wrist...and, he was pretty sure, nothing else.

In that moment, a strange sense of inevitability settled over him.

"So...waiting for someone to join you?" he managed to say, noticing *six* champagne bottles lined up on the edge of the hot tub. Corks littered the floor and the room smelled like champagne. A single crystal flute rested next to her, filled with the sparkling, straw-colored vintage. "Brooks, maybe?" He made his voice casual and easy, but the very thought sent a shaft of deep, dark anger shooting through him. *Better get the hell out of here, Wilder.*

"Hell no," she replied. To his consternation, she seemed utterly at ease. It blew his frigging mind. "But, you know...it could've been you, Johnny Wilder." She lifted the flute in a silent toast, then drank.

"Right." The single syllable came out low and barely audible. Because by now, he was seriously thinking about getting out of his clothes and joining her. He looked away and his eyes fell on her shimmery red dress, along with an unidentifiable flesh-colored article of clothing that wasn't a bra, a sparkling handbag, and her tall, elegant gold shoes. "You going to leave those there all night?"

"There are robes here. This is the spa, you know," she said, gesturing to a fluffy one hanging over a chair on the other side. "Besides, I'm not putting those damn Spanx on again tonight—and I can't get back in my dress without them."

"Spanks?" Finally, he understood. That nude-colored thing must be some sort of undergarment. He couldn't hold back a grin. "My mom claims it takes her ten minutes to get hers on. Is that normal?"

She hooted in delight, a big belly laugh. Her nose crinkled up and her eyes lit and her beautiful, lipstick-free mouth was wide and filled with merriment. Wilder felt a wave of something sad and hot and uncomfortable rush over him... especially when she moved sharply and he caught a hint of breast bobbing beneath the rumbling water.

"I don't know what's normal, but it's a pain in the ass. I heard, though, that Beyonce wears *two* pairs," she told him, still laughing.

"So...what's with the gun?" he said, settling on the edge of the hot tub a safe distance away...but next to where her red-painted toenails occasionally bobbed to the surface. *Do not think about what else is below that water.* "And what are you doing here? Alone?"

"Grab a glass," she said, making a gesture toward the kitchen. "I'll tell you the whole sordid story. But let me start by saying: My Damned Aunt Helen!"

He vaguely remembered the iron-haired lady with the sharp fingernails and violent walking stick. In fact, he'd seen her and his mother in animated conversation shortly after midnight, just as he and an irate Laney were leaving. Something nudged the back of his mind, but he put it away for now. Much more important things at hand. Like keeping his wits about him.

Instead of going to get a glass, he reached for the nearest open bottle of champagne. It was empty. He started to grab the next one, but she waved him off.

"They're all empty except this one," she said, gesturing to the one beside her.

"My God, did you drink them all?" She should be loaded.

"No," she giggled. "I poured them in here. I've always wanted a champagne bath. Bubbling bubbly!"

He couldn't hold back his own laugh. "Tess...my God, you are a piece of work."

"That's what I'm told." She waved again. "There were a lot left over this year because everyone went home early—and I used the cheaper ones, not the fifty-dollar ones. Daddy won't care." She grinned cheekily. "He's just happy to have me home. I'm stuck here, so I might as well celebrate."

"Celebrate what?"

"A new life. My divorce. Leaving the stage. Doing something that *means* something—to me." She was beaming and glowing, clearly at peace with herself...and he felt something shift inside, at his core...just as it had years ago. *Ka-blam.*

Only this time he knew what it meant. That sense of kismet prickled at him. "So what are you still doing here? Are you going to tell me or what? You can never get to the point, can you?"

"Sure, but...first, what are you doing here? Why aren't you with your...*very sexy date*?" She said these last few words in a breathy, teasing whisper, then waggled her eyebrows.

"As it happens," he said, thinking even more seriously about getting out of his clothes and sliding into the hot, rumbling water, "she saw something that pissed her off quite a bit."

"Oh dear." Tess clearly tried to adopt a sober expression, but a glint of levity danced in her eyes. "Did she see you manhandling me up against the wall, kissing the shit out of me? Or was it someone else you were mauling?"

"Jesus, Tess," he breathed, "are you sure you didn't drink

all those bottles of champagne?" His pulse was pounding and other parts of him, which had been more than mildly interested in the situation, rocketed to attention. *So I kissed the shit out of her, did I?*

"Well, that's what you did. Quite effectively I might add. Cheers." She lifted her glass then shook her head. "If you'd played your cards right, you might be in here" —she splashed the water with a firm hand, giving him a flash of breast— "right now."

"So," he said, thinking of the old J. Geils song "Trying Not to Think About It", "I took her home. It wasn't a very pleasant drive."

"No. I'm sure it wasn't."

"Then I got home and my mom sent me back out in this frigging mess to come and get the mink stole that she left here."

Tess raised her brows and her nose crinkled. "I didn't see any mink stoles, and I was looking all over the place...because I couldn't find my purse. That's why *I'm* here."

"Isn't that your bag over there?"

"*No,*" she said with a flash of exasperation. "That's my Aunt Helen's pocketbook. That's the problem. I think she must have taken mine by mistake, because they look similar. And the old bat has bad eyesight, even though she claims she doesn't. Mine had not only my keys, but also my cell phone in it. So I couldn't call anyone to come and get me when I realized I didn't have my keys."

"But—are you telling me whoever was here at the end *left* you without walking you out to your car?" He was outraged. "Who the hell would leave a woman here alone on a night like this?"

She looked at him seriously. "I know, right?" She rolled her eyes. "It was Ringlee, the lead singer—he was hot to get home with his latest groupie, and he thought I was right behind him. I thought I was too until I got outside and realized I didn't have the right handbag. But at least I did have this." She picked up the petite gun, waving it around energetically. "Apparently, since she helped solve a murder back home in Maine, Aunt Helen fancies herself quite the detective."

"Right," he drawled. "You do know that's not a real gun."

She rolled her eyes. "Of course I do. But you didn't until you got a closer look at it, and what else was I going to do? Stuck here alone? Anyone could have come in."

"But why didn't you call from the Club's phone? Or is the line down from the ice storm?"

"No, I called...but. Well. I don't actually know anyone's cell phone numbers—they're all in my phone. The only number I know by heart is Mom and Dad's home phone. And Aunt Helen answered and all I could hear was her screeching 'What? I can't hear you! Speak up! The lines must be screwy!' I called a couple times, but the same thing happened. So I figured...I'm stranded here overnight, but at least I have champagne and food...and a hot tub."

"Right."

Her foot, its nails painted bloodred with some kind of sparkly stuff on top, slipped out of the water and settled on the edge next to him. It was an elegant foot, smooth and feminine and quite tiny in relation to his. And there was one small freckle, right at the base between the big toe and the first toe. Very unexpected. And ridiculously sexy.

Before he quite realized what he was doing, Wilder

curled his fingers around that warm foot. "Ticklish?" he asked, glancing at her...and looking at the very nice calf that was now out of the water.

"Not a bit," she replied, sinking down lower so the water covered her shoulders and most of her neck. The stem of her glass was submerged in the raging water and she was watching him with those dark brown eyes...just watching.

The moment was surreal to him...something he'd fantasized about for a decade...and yet it no longer seemed so important. Or desperate. Or...earth-shattering.

It simply felt...*right*. As if some cosmic thing had happened to shift his world, his perception.

Hell. Maybe he *had* broken the damned curse. He smoothed his hand along the gentle curve of her instep, unable to keep from touching her now that he'd started. He caught up her foot, positioning it so the sole faced him and used his thumbs to massage the bottom.

"Mmm...." she sighed, setting her glass on the edge and closing her eyes. "So what's this about a curse?"

CHAPTER 12

TESS COULDN'T REMEMBER EVER BEING SO turned on.

From the gentle buzz from the champagne to the heat of the bubbly charging up around her, dancing over her breasts and teasing her nipples, to the fact that she was completely naked and a man she'd lusted after for years was completely dressed...and massaging her foot....She was a live wire.

What the hell did she have to do to get him to join her?

She'd had to put her glass aside for fear it would fall from her nerveless fingers. He made her mouth water and her hormones ping.

And Wilder was just sitting there, on the edge of the tub, massaging her foot, carrying on a conversation as if they'd met on the street. Still in his evening clothes, he appeared relaxed—deliciously rumpled and disordered. His white shirt had splashes on it from the hot tub and the sleeves were rolled up to expose muscular arms. He'd unbuttoned the top two buttons, revealing a vee of dark hair and the curve of his throat. He must have shaved this morning, because the stubble was already darkening the fine, square jaw.

"The curse?" He glanced over at her, his gray eyes contemplative. "You're the curse."

"Me?" That threw her for a loop. "How so?"

He released her foot and it slid back into the water as he rose and walked over to pick up her glass. Now he was standing behind her, so she had to tip her head back and look over. *Why won't he take off his damn shirt?*

He took a drink then refilled the flute from the last bottle she'd brought in here and set it back down next to her. "Has it occurred to you that for the last ten years, we've been... together, or otherwise in touch, on just about every New Year's Eve?"

She thought about that, thought about the last few years. "Well, there was that first one—when we first started the bet. When I kissed you."

"Yes." His voice was hardly more than a breath. "That was the beginning of it. Ever since then, you've totally ruined my New Year's Eves."

She nearly surged up out of the water in disbelief, but caught herself at the last minute. Even though it was getting hot in the tub, she felt a little awkward about exposing herself. This was Johnny Wilder, but this was a different Johnny Wilder than she remembered.

Different from the one who thought of her as intimidating. Who texted suggestive comments instead of whispering them in her ear.

No doubt about it: he'd changed. *Oh*, he'd changed. He'd become a man.

And she realized...*I want this man.* This gallant, brave,

sensitive man who'd risked his life for his country but would kiss his mother's feet if she asked him to. Who'd been in her life...but not quite visible enough, not quite assertively enough...for ten years.

She collected her thoughts, drawing in a long, slow breath...just enough to lift the tops of her breasts from beneath the rumbling water. When she saw his eyes go right there, and his knuckles turn white, she knew there was still more than a chance.

"So, I've ruined your New Year's Eves. Want to explain further?"

"Well, there was that first one. And then the year after, we all hung out—you and me and Grat and Cara and my date and your date. And that was fine. But I remembered that kiss, you know."

"Yeah. I think you're exaggerating. How did I ruin that one particularly?"

"Well, I blame you for the fact that I haven't gotten laid on New Year's Eve for ten years. Including that one. At the time, I didn't know it was because of the Curse of Tess Devine, but now in retrospect....And then the year after," he said, raising his voice to be heard over her protests, "we were here all night—remember? With the flood? I sent Kaylie Schwartz and her 34 double-Ds home alone and came in to help you. You blew my mind that night, you know—out here in your evening gown and boots. You could've been home in bed...but you were here. Working."

"Of course I remember. That was...that was one of my fondest memories. And you were here too, of your own volition. And you know...I almost kissed you that night. When you dropped me off at home? I was just about to lean in, then

I thought...no. He's not interested. He's dating Kaylie. And I was afraid I'd ruin our friendship—which I really did enjoy."

The look of consternation on his face was a balm to the fact that she'd just made that confession. "Well, that sucks. Because I was trying to work up the nerve to do the same thing." He sat on the edge of the tub, looking down at her, his feet on the floor.

"What about the year I asked *you* out? How could I have ruined your night?" she demanded, her mouth suddenly dry. His hand was right there, propped on the edge next to her, showing off a strong, sturdy wrist and muscled arm. "You blew me off."

He nodded. "Yeah. I just didn't want to see you, Tess. It was too difficult...especially since you never seemed to respond to my overtures."

"Your texting overtures? Really? You were totally drunk that night—you probably don't even remember what you said to me. How was I supposed to take you seriously? Or the year...the night...you know," she felt her cheeks warm. "The night you stayed at my parents' house. You were smashed. You were saying all sorts of things...you probably don't remember any of it. And it's just as well I didn't fall for it. I know you were just trying to get in my pants. It's what you do. You're an opportunist. I know that about you." Which was why she really couldn't believe anything he said. "You were going off to the service, I was getting married—it was a last-ditch effort. But I knew that." *I wanted to believe you, but I knew better.*

"Tess," he said, his voice a low, careful drawl. "I remember everything I've ever said to you. Or texted you." His gray eyes held hers and she suddenly couldn't breathe—

his gaze was deep and intense and hot. Something deep inside her quivered, sharp and hard. "And I meant it."

Then he quirked a cocky grin, his eyelids sliding half closed, his voice dropping even lower. "Trust me, if I'd *just* been trying to get in your pants...I would have."

Tess looked up at him, aware of all sorts of crystalline pieces settling into place in the back of her mind. "The problem is," she managed to say, even though her heart was racing and her pulse had spiked and she felt as if she were about to make some great reveal, "I know you too well...I know how you are with women. I know better. And it's okay. So why don't you climb on in here with me and let's see how *amazing* we could be together. It's been ten years...let's finish it."

His eyes glittered. "Not interested in that, Tess. I might have been once, but not anymore."

Her lungs seized up, tightened, and she couldn't breathe. Her vision turned dark with mortification. Her lips formed a half-smile that she tried to make cool and collected, but inside she was reeling. "All right then," she managed. "Consider the curse broken."

"You don't understand. I'm in love with you, Tess." He said it in that low, sexy drawl.

But he was looking at her, and the words were clear—and this time she knew she'd heard it correctly. But he repeated it, taking her hand and putting it to his chest where his heart thumped madly. "I'm *in love with you*. But I'm no longer intimidated by you. I'm no longer afraid to say it. Being at war changes a man. You learn what's important and to go after what you want—no settling for second best. For left-overs or after thoughts. And so...if I climb in that tub...I expect to spend every New Year with you for the rest of our lives."

"Then what," she said, reaching for his shirt, "the *hell* are you still doing up...there?" And she pulled him toward her, down to kiss her—and he came easily—and then, in a long, slow movement, down into the water.

When their lips parted, damp and hot from the steamy water, she looked into his eyes. "So can you stop calling me your curse now?" she asked, sliding her hand down along a very solid belly to the very interesting package behind his zipper. *Oh yes.* She grinned, exploring behind his wet trousers.

He sighed, the cords of his neck tightening as she found him and cupped him with her fingers. "Right," Wilder said, dipping his mouth to nuzzle a spot right next to the hollow of her throat. "My curse...and my blessing. Happy New Year, Tess."

"Happy New Year, my love."

Don't let announcements and news get stuck in
your spam folder!
Sign up for SMS/Text messages and help keep your inbox
clear!

Just type in 38470 for the phone number,
and then type COLLEEN in the message space!

ABOUT THE AUTHOR

Colleen Gleason is an award-winning, New York Times and USA Today best-selling author. She's written more than forty novels in a variety of genres—truly, something for everyone!

She loves to hear from readers, so feel free to find her online.

Get SMS/Text alerts for any
New Releases or **Promotions!**

Text: **COLLEEN** to **38470**

(You will only receive a single message when Colleen has a new release or title on sale. *We promise.*)

If you would like SMS/Text alerts for any **Events** or book signings Colleen is attending,

Text: **MEET** to **38470**

Subscribe to Colleen's non-spam newsletter for other
updates, news, sneak peeks, and special offers!
http://cgbks.com/news

Connect with Colleen online:
www.colleengleason.com
books@colleengleason.com

The Gardella Vampire Hunters

Victoria

The Rest Falls Away

Rises the Night

The Bleeding Dusk

When Twilight Burns

As Shadows Fade

Macey & Max Denton

Roaring Midnight

Raging Dawn

Roaring Shadows

Raging Winter

Roaring Dawn

The Draculia Vampires

Dark Rogue: The Vampire Voss

Dark Saint: The Vampire Dimitri

Dark Vixen: The Vampire Narcise

Vampire at Sea: Tales from the Draculia Vampires

Wicks Hollow Series
Ghost Story Romance & Mystery

Sinister Summer

Sinister Secrets

Sinister Shadows

Sinister Sanctuary

Sinister Stage

Sinister Lang Syne

Stoker & Holmes Books

(for ages 12-adult)

The Clockwork Scarab

The Spiritglass Charade

The Chess Queen Enigma

The Carnelian Crow

The Zeppelin Deception

The Lincoln's White House Mystery Series

(writing as C. M. Gleason)

Murder in the Lincoln White House

Murder in the Oval Library

Murder at the Capitol

The Marina Alexander Adventure Novels

(writing as C. M. Gleason)

Siberian Treasure

Amazon Roulette

Sanskrit Cipher (coming 2021!)

Writing as Alex Mandon

The Belle-Époque Mystery series

Murder on the Champs-Élysées

www.ingramcontent.com/pod-product-compliance
Lightning Source LLC
Chambersburg PA
CBHW071255190726
48292CB00007B/2550